GRAVE DOUBT

GRAVE DOUBT

Michael Allegretto

Carroll & Graf Publishers, Inc.
New York

First printing 1995

Carroll & Graf Publishers, Inc.
260 Fifth Avenue
New York, NY 10001

Library of Congress Cataloging-in-Publication Data

Allegretto, Michael.
    Grave doubt / Michael Allegretto.
        p.   cm.
    ISBN 0-7867-0186-2
    I. Title.
PS3551.L385G73   1995
813'.54—dc20   95-10407
                                          CIP

Manufactured in the United States of America

GRAVE DOUBT

1

"My wife has been getting phone calls from her first husband," Roger Armis told me.

"Threatening calls?"

"You might say that. He's been dead for four years."

Armis sat in the visitor's chair across the desk from me. He *looked* like a reasonable man—early fifties, expensively cut gray hair, lightweight summer suit, also gray, with an off-white shirt and a pale blue tie. But looks can be deceiving. I once had a client who could pass for a bank president, and he claimed aliens were beaming radio waves through his toilet. Armis, by the way, was a banker, too. But only a branch manager.

"You did say dead."

"I know it sounds crazy," he said.

"Has your wife seen this man?"

"No. He's phoned Vivian half a dozen times in the past few weeks. But she's convinced it's him."

"Did she recognize his voice?"

Armis nodded. "And he told her ... certain things that only the two of them could know."

"Such as?"

His face flushed slightly. "Intimate things."

"Sex, you mean."

He nodded tightly. He was too much of a gentleman to speak of such matters. A lot of guys, though, weren't.

"Isn't it possible her first husband discussed the, ah, details of his sex life with his drinking buddies, and that it's one of these characters who's been calling, perhaps disguising his voice?"

"That was my first thought," Armis said. "But Vivian says definitely not. She tested him with specific questions. There's no doubt in her mind. This man is her first husband."

"Back from the dead."

Armis shifted in his seat. "It would seem."

"I assume your wife is . . . of sound mind."

"Yes, of course," he said with some impatience.

I got out a legal pad and a pen. "All right, let's back up a little. What's her first husband's name?"

"Martin Blyleven."

"How did he die?"

"In a plane crash. A small plane, just he and the pilot were on board."

"Where?"

"In Arizona. He was flying from here to Tucson on business."

"Did your wife identify the body?"

"No. Blyleven and the pilot were burned beyond recognition in the crash. But the police said there was no doubt it was them."

"What did they match, fingerprints or dental records?"

"I don't know which. But Martin Blyleven was pronounced officially dead. The FAA, the insurance companies, everyone agreed. There was a funeral, and his remains lie in a grave in Crown Hill Cemetery. And now he's . . . come back."

"But, of course, it can't be him."

Armis hesitated. "No, of course not."

"You don't seem entirely certain."

He heaved a sigh. "Logically, this man can't be Blyleven. On the other hand, I can't ignore Vivian's beliefs. She's a sensible, practical woman, not given to hysteria or wild imagination. And she is one hundred percent convinced that this man is Martin Blyleven."

"I see. And why exactly is he calling now after being *gone* for four years?"

"He wants money. Four hundred thousand dollars. We have to have it by next Monday, a week from today."

"Or else what?"

"If we refuse to pay he'll come forward, present himself to the authorities, and explain that he was never on that plane and that he's been suffering from amnesia for all these years." Armis gave a small shrug. "If it truly is him, Vivian would have to pay back the insurance premium in the amount of—"

"Let me guess. Four hundred thousand."

"Yes. One way or the other, we'd have to pay."

"Blackmail, pure and simple."

"It's not so simple. He also threatens to demand joint custody of his daughter."

"Oh?"

"Chelsea was a year and a half old at the time of the plane crash. After Vivian and I were married, I adopted Chelsea, and now she carries my name. As far as I'm concerned, she's my daughter. But the courts would probably grant Blyleven at least visitation rights. And he hinted to Vivian that an accident could happen while Chelsea was with him."

"Have you talked to the police about this?"

"No."

"Then I suggest we call them now and—"

"Absolutely not. If there is the slightest hint of police involvement, he'll come forward."

"Let him. He can't possibly be Blyleven."

"I . . . I don't know *who* he is. And until I'm certain, I want this handled in the strictest confidence. Now, I told my attorney that I needed a private investigator—without telling him why—and he recommended you. He said you were 'effective and discreet.' " Armis glanced around my office. "I suppose I can trust his judgment."

Apparently, he was not impressed with the decor—worn wooden desk and chairs, preowned leather couch, no-frills file cabinets, and Venetian-blind-covered windows that looked down on Broadway. It was after nine A.M., so there was little traffic below. The office was cool and quiet. This afternoon, though, when the July sun swung over to the west side of the street, you could bake bread out on the windowsill. That is, if you didn't mind a fine layer of pollution on the crust.

"There's another possible explanation here," I said. "One that's difficult to broach."

"Yes?"

"Your wife and this man could be in on it together."

His mouth opened, then snapped closed. "That is out of the question."

"I only offer it as a—"

"It's *quite* impossible." Color had risen to his cheeks. "Vivian would be incapable of doing anything like that, do you understand?"

"Sure."

His jaws were clenched and his lips were pressed tightly together. I could tell that he'd considered the possibility.

He drew a deep breath and let it out. "Besides," he said, "she didn't volunteer this information. In fact, she was trying to put together the blackmail money without my knowledge. When I found out that she'd emptied her personal bank account and was trying to sell her jewelry, I pressed her for an explanation. That's when she told me."

I wasn't ready to discount the possibility of his wife's complicity. But I let it go for now.

"How long have you and Vivian been married?"

"Nearly three years. When we met, I'd been divorced for some time—all my children had grown up and my wife wanted to stop being a wife and start being a career woman. Vivian and Chelsea were so sweet that I realized how much I missed having a family, being a father, and so on. We were married shortly after we met. I guess she needed someone, too. And I must tell you, Mr. Lomax, that despite the fifteen-year difference in our ages, we make one another very happy. All three of us."

I could see that he meant it.

"I'll be honest with you," he said. "If I thought this man would leave us alone, I would pay him off."

"With the insurance money?"

He smiled without humor and shook his head. "We no longer have that money. Soon after we were married, Vivian's mother was diagnosed with cancer. She'd let her medical insurance lapse, and so Vivian and I paid for everything—two major surgeries, chemotherapy, and radiation treatments. She was bedridden in a private room for two years before she died. Now she's gone and so is the four hundred thousand. Vivian and I would have to sell off all of our assets and borrow the rest. It would put us deeply in debt, a hardship for all three of us.'' He paused. ''But it could be done.''

''I'd advise against it. What's to keep this man from demanding more?''

''Precisely,'' he said. ''A month from now, or five years from now, he could put us through this again. One way or the other, I want to resolve it now.''

''How?''

''I was hoping you would know.''

''Yes, well, the first thing we should do is verify that Martin Blyleven couldn't possibly be alive. I'll start with the insurance company.''

''Pioneer Insurance,'' he said.

''After that, we can try to identify the blackmailer. I'll need your wife's help for that.''

''No,'' he said quickly.

''Excuse me?''

''We, ah, we can't tell Vivian about this. About your involvement, I mean.''

I waited. He shifted uneasily in his chair.

''You see . . . Vivian wants to pay. She believes that Martin— or whoever he is—will simply go away. In fact, she thinks that right now I'm out trying to put together the money. She's terrified, on the edge of a breakdown. She told me she'd run away with Chelsea before she'd let Blyleven get his hands on her. If she knew you were involved, I . . . I don't know what she'd do.''

His face was pale and he sat rigidly in his chair. If anyone was on the verge of a breakdown, it was him.

As gently as I could, I said, ''Mr. Armis, don't you think it's unfair to your wife for us to scheme behind her back?''

''I . . .'' He swallowed and shook his head.

''It's essential that I talk to her,'' I said. ''I need to know exactly how this man could so convincingly pass himself off as her first husband.''

"I've already told you.''

"In so many words. I need to hear it from her. Whoever he is, he has to be someone who was close to Blyleven. Your wife can probably help us narrow it down.''

He nodded. "All right.'' His voice was small. "When can you begin?''

"I already have.''

We discussed my fee, and he wrote out a check. Then he stood to leave.

I said, "Hypothetically, what if this man really is Martin Blyleven?''

"It . . . can't be him.''

"I suppose not,'' I said. Although he hadn't answered my question.

2

After Armis left, I phoned Pioneer Insurance. I was shuffled around for a while, until I finally got what I wanted—the name of the investigator who had worked on Martin Blyleven's plane crash.

I called him, and he agreed to see me.

I locked up the office and headed out.

On the second floor with me is a vacancy, a dentist who I wouldn't let inside my home much less my mouth, and Acme, Inc. In the four-plus years that I've worked in this building, I'd never seen Mr. Acme. I didn't even know what line of work he was in. But he was always on the phone. He was on it now as I passed by his door.

"... goddamn strings, Murray. Twelve hundred rackets you send me, and none of them are strung. Who do I sell them to, mimes? Or are they playing tennis now with beachballs? Because that's the smallest thing you could hit, Murray, without any goddamn ..."

The morning was already heating up as I steered the old Olds across town to Lakewood, which lies just beyond the southwest reach of Denver. A thin veil of smog partially obscured the mountains to the west, making them flat and featureless. By this afternoon you might not see them at all.

Warwick Investigations had been in business for ten years, about twice as long as I had. The difference was, these guys knew how to make money. They did a lot of corporate work—checking employees' backgrounds, designing building security, consulting retailers on methods to reduce shoplifting, and investigating large insurance claims—none of the nickel-and-dime stuff.

Thank God, or I'd be out of work.

They had the top floor of a three-story, steel-and-glass building near Hampden Avenue and Wadsworth Boulevard. I put on my jacket, straightened my tie, and stepped off the elevator.

A young, attractive, blue-eyed receptionist in a clinging beige dress showed me in to see the man himself, Donald Warwick.

Theoretically, Warwick and I were in the same business. But you'd never know it from his office. The furnishings were dark blue and beige, the same shades, in fact, as the receptionist out front. There were tasteful prints on the walls and thick, off-white carpeting underfoot. A cluster of low-slung chairs surrounded a table in one corner, nearly out of earshot from Warwick's gleaming desk.

Beyond the desk was a work area featuring not one, but two computers, both switched on, their screens filled with colorful, cryptic blocks of words and numbers, no doubt critical data for the state-of-the-art detective. There was also a printer, a fax machine, and a copy machine. The telephone on Warwick's desk had half a dozen buttons, four of which were blinking. More calls than I got in a week.

If Donald Warwick was a private investigator, what the hell was I?

"It's nice to meet you," he said.

He was a small man with an intense stare and a cool, dry handshake. He wore steel-rimmed glasses, a tan Armani suit, and a fifty-dollar haircut.

"I've heard about you," he added.

"You're kidding."

"Not at all." He motioned me into a visitor's chair and sat behind his desk. I waited for him to explain what he'd heard or where he'd heard it. But he merely inquired, "May I ask what your interest is in the Blyleven case?"

"I've been hired by a Canadian insurance company," I lied, keeping Roger and Vivian Armis out of it. "They're holding a policy on Blyleven's life, and the beneficiary is a distant cousin living in Montreal. Because of a clerical error, they've only recently learned of Blyleven's death. They hired me to assemble the facts on the plane crash. It's mostly a formality. You know how these insurance companies are.''

He gave me a half-smile that said, ''You bet I do.'' Or maybe he was merely amused by my bullshit. Whatever the case, he had his secretary bring him the file on Blyleven.

I had expected a couple of pages. The file was an inch thick. Apparently, Roger Armis had left out a few details.

''How much do you know about this case?''

''Next to nothing,'' I admitted.

He took off his glasses, whipped out a handkerchief with a flourish, and wiped them until they gleamed.

''Feel free to take notes,'' he said, carefully replacing his glasses. ''Much of this is public information. But I can't give you copies of any of these reports. Company policy. I'm sure you understand.''

I didn't, but I said, ''Sure.'' Besides, he wasn't charging me for his time—professional courtesy.

First he gave me Martin Blyleven's date and place of birth and his social security number to make sure we were talking about the same person. He even had a picture of him, a three-by-five color shot from the chest up. Blyleven's face was triangular with a pointed chin, narrow nose, and wide-set brown eyes. His hair, also brown, was parted on the side. He wore a blue suit, and he smiled woodenly at the camera.

Warwick said, ''Mr. Blyleven was employed by the Reverend Franklin Reed as his chief accountant. He—''

''Excuse me. Is that the TV preacher Franklin Reed? The one in south Denver?''

''Yes. Blyleven worked for Reed for several years. He often flew to Tucson on business. You see, the church has several concerns down there—a large retirement community and an organization called World Flock, which aids people in impoverished countries.''

Warwick flipped a page, studied it for a moment, then flipped another one.

"On March eighteenth, four years ago, Blyleven boarded a plane owned by the church, a twin-engine four-seater. There were no other passengers, just the pilot, Lawrence Foster."

"Was Foster also employed by the church?"

Warwick nodded and said, "They left Centennial Airport at four-ten P.M. bound for Tucson International. The flight usually took about four hours, depending on the wind currents. Of course, this time they never arrived. An air search was initiated, and two days later a pilot from the Civil Air Patrol spotted part of the wreckage in the Fort Apache Indian Reservation, about a hundred miles northeast of Phoenix. Investigators from the FAA and the National Transportation Safety Board took a week to find all the pieces."

"Why so long?"

"The area is remote, and the wreckage was scattered over several square miles."

"So the plane broke up in the air."

"It didn't break up. It blew up."

"What do you mean, a malfunction?"

He shook his head. "A bomb."

"What?"

"According to the FBI, it was some type of military explosive, probably C-4. The aircraft was literally blown out of the sky in a thousand fiery pieces, some of them human. Only parts of the two bodies were recovered, all badly burned."

I wondered why Roger Armis hadn't told me any of this. Maybe Vivian hadn't told him.

"How were the bodies identified?"

"Lawrence Foster was positively ID'd through dental records."

"What about Blyleven?"

"There wasn't enough of him left to make a positive ID, but the circumstantial evidence was strong. Pieces of leg and arm bones fit his age and size. They also found his wedding ring, part of a shoe, even the keys to his house and car."

"Why couldn't they get a dental match?"

"After they'd pieced together the remains of the aircraft and the bodies, the FBI determined that the point of explosion was behind the rearmost seats and in proximity to Mr. Blyleven's face, as if he were sitting on the floor holding the explosives. They found little of his head.''

"Wait a minute. Are you saying he held a bomb to his face and then set it off?''

He pursed his lips and turned his hands palms up. ''That's one explanation. Or else the bomb went off accidentally. Or perhaps it was in a sealed package and he didn't know what he was holding. There were plenty of theories kicked around. Pioneer Insurance, frankly, was hoping for suicide.''

"So they wouldn't have to pay the widow.''

"Exactly. As it was, they had to pay double. Death by misadventure. In fact, as a matter of routine, they had me investigate her. But nothing ever came of that.''

"What did the feds finally determine?''

"They didn't. As far as I know, the case remains unsolved. They weren't able to conclude who put the explosives on the plane—Blyleven, Foster, or a third party.''

I could see that Roger Armis had coaxed me into the shallow end of a pool. It got deeper with each step.

"What about motive?''

"The police, the FBI, and my agency all performed extensive background checks. As far as we could tell, neither Blyleven nor Foster had any enemies, anyone who would want to harm them, much less have the means or opportunity to rig up a bomb on the plane. Nor could we find a reason for suicide. Neither of the men was depressed or under stress, and they each left behind a wife and a small child.'' He spread his hands and gave me his half-smile. ''A mystery, Mr. Lomax.''

Perhaps more so than he knew.

"Did anyone ever suggest that the unidentified body might not be Blyleven?''

"It *was* identified.''

"But not by fingerprints or dental records. Isn't it possible that the man with Foster wasn't Blyleven?''

"No, it is not possible.''

"Maybe someone who *resembled* Blyleven got on the plane.''

He sighed to let me know that he dealt in facts, not fantasy. "At least three people saw Mr. Blyleven and Mr. Foster board the plane. These people knew Blyleven personally. They spoke to him. Do you understand? It was him. The plane took off, and a few hours later it blew up with him on board.''

''Perhaps a third party was hiding on the plane before it took off, and sometime later Blyleven bailed out.''

Warwick was shaking his head. ''Not a chance. We've examined that possibility and every other one you could dream up. The plane was checked inside and out the evening before the flight. There were no hidden bombs or parachutes, much less *people* on board. And the plane was locked in a hangar overnight with a guard on duty. We have signed affidavits from all of these people.''

''What are their names?''

He sighed and told me.

I said, ''Maybe the plane landed somewhere, and Blyleven got off and someone else got on.''

''Landed where? In the middle of the desert? And for what purpose? So that Blyleven could switch places with some unknown third party, who would then obligingly blow himself up? And all this with the full cooperation of the pilot, who would also be blown to bits?''

He had a point. Still ... ''It's possible, though, right?''

He gave me an irritated look. ''It's also possible that Elvis is alive and well and impersonating Wayne Newton. But I wouldn't bet my money *or* my reputation on it.''

He closed the file with authority.

''If your Canadian insurance company is looking for a way to avoid paying the beneficiary, Mr. Lomax, they'll have to look somewhere else. Martin Blyleven died in that crash.''

Maybe so. But lately he'd been phoning his wife.

3

I fired up the Olds and headed toward Centennial Airport.

My original plan had been to confirm Blyleven's death and then try to identify the impostor who'd phoned Vivian Armis.

But now I wasn't so sure there was an impostor. The proof of Blyleven's death was merely charred body parts and circumstantial evidence.

Of course, any judge will tell you that circumstantial evidence is *evidence,* every bit as valid as direct evidence. The example they like to give is this: Before you go to bed at night you look out the window and see that your lawn is green. In the morning your yard is covered with a foot of cold, wet, white stuff. From this circumstantial evidence you can conclude beyond a reasonable doubt that it *snowed* during the night, even though you didn't actually see snowflakes fall from the sky. Case closed.

What they fail to mention is that it's *possible* that while you were asleep, a neighbor trucked in a snow machine from one of the ski areas . . . and so on.

So Blyleven could be alive. Theoretically.

Warwick and the federal investigators had considered this possibility. Pioneer Insurance had been especially suspicious. Why not? They'd had to cough up four hundred grand.

But if Blyleven was alive, then a couple dozen questions came to mind, the main one being, How had he arranged a stand-in for the midair explosion?

Also, why had he done it?

Where had he been for four years?

Why had he waited until now to return?

And why would he try to blackmail his own widow, er, wife?

Blyleven aside, Roger and Vivian Armis had to deal with a blackmailer, no matter who he was. If it were up to me, I'd leave the money for the guy, and when he came to pick it up, I'd jump out of a tree and land on his back. But it wasn't up to me. As far as Roger and Vivian were concerned, it made all the difference in the world whether the blackmailer was Blyleven. So that's what I had to find out.

There were several directions I could go. Of course, highly trained federal snoops and high-tech PIs had scoured the ground before me. It was doubtful I'd find anything new. But I had little choice.

Well, I did have one choice. Give back my fee to Armis.

However, I was not moved to do this, for two very good reasons. First, the man had come to me for help and I'd agreed to help him. And second, my present bank account could fit in a derelict's ear with room left over for the wax.

One thing I had going for me: if Blyleven had faked his death, he'd taken elaborate steps to do so, and somebody must have noticed *something*. Also, if he was alive, then he'd been *somewhere* for the past four years. And unless he'd been hiding in a cave and eating roots and insects, somebody had seen him and talked to him, even if it was only when he'd come into town for supplies.

I intended to question Vivian as soon as her husband broke the disturbing news: Lomax is here. In the meantime, I'd talk to the last people who had seen Blyleven alive.

Airport personnel.

Centennial Airport caters to private aircraft and some charter flights. It straddles the line between Arapahoe and Douglas counties, just beyond the southeastern fringe of the suburban sprawl. The area is mostly rolling plains and native grass. Buffalo country, you might say. A few stone-and-glass office parks are encamped here and there, like outposts, waiting for the settlers to arrive. And they will, too, you can bet your real-estate license on that.

The airport itself is bordered by a few dozen flat-roofed offices and hangars, which all look pretty much alike, except the offices have windows. The control tower rises above them like an exclamation point.

I parked in the lot and watched a tiny red plane climb slowly in the distance, like a kite on a string.

I asked around for Chris Esteves and Thomas Doherty, two names Warwick had given me. No one seemed to know Esteves. But someone pointed out a hangar and told me Doherty worked there.

The massive structure was cool and dim and smelled faintly of machine oil. Half a dozen small planes were arranged wing to wing and nose to tail, as shiny and bright as new toys. There was a guy standing on a step stool beside a blue-and-white aircraft, monkeying around with the engine. Part of the cowling lay on the cement floor beside a chest-high metal tool cabinet on wheels.

"Excuse me, Thomas Doherty?"

"That's me," he said, without turning around. He tightened a bolt with a socket wrench.

"Could I talk to you for a minute?"

He fitted the wrench on another bolt head. "About what?"

"Martin Blyleven."

He hesitated, then stepped down off the stool and wiped the wrench with a rag. He was a goofy-looking character with buck teeth, jug ears, a walnut-size Adam's apple, and a mop of red hair. His eyes were slightly crossed, giving the impression that he was staring at something behind me. I resisted the urge to look over my shoulder.

I handed him my card. "An insurance company hired me to look into the crash that killed Martin Blyleven and Lawrence Foster."

His face drooped a bit. "Larry was a helluva good guy. Damn good pilot, too." He shook his head sadly. "A crying shame, what happened."

"How well did you know Blyleven?"

"I knew him to say hello. He seemed like an okay guy."

"You were here the day of the accident, right?"

"Yep."

"It was a long time ago, I realize, but do you remember what happened that day?"

"Sure. I told the story often enough to the authorities."

"What time did you come to work?"

"Seven A.M., like always."

"Was Blyleven's plane outside or in a hangar?"

"His church's plane, you mean. It was right here in this hangar. I'd made some adjustments to the rudder controls the day before. Larry told me they were feeling tight, and it took me all day to find the problem."

"So you worked on the plane the day *before* the flight."

"That's right."

"Did you go into the cabin?"

"I had to, sure."

"See anything out of the ordinary?"

"The authorities asked me that. No."

"Could someone have been hiding on the plane without you seeing them?"

His eyes widened, one aimed at my nose, the other somewhere past my left ear. "Why would anybody want to do that?"

"I don't know. But is it physically possible?"

"No way. I mean, on that model there are storage compartments behind the rearmost seats, to stow gear and so on, and I suppose a person could squeeze in there. But the compartments were empty. The doors were open."

"Any parachutes in there."

"*Nothing* was in there."

"Could someone have snuck inside after you worked on the plane?"

He shook his head no. "I was the last one to leave the hangar that night, and that plane was the last thing I checked. The hangar was locked tight overnight. *And*—" he emphasized, before I could ask him another question, "—I was the first one here in the morning. Early. The night watchman let me in."

"Did you check out the plane again?"

"No, I was finished with it."

"What's the watchman's name?"

"Earl Wilson."

"Does he still work here?"

"He retired a few years back and moved down to Castle Rock. Anyway, I was here all day, and no one went near that plane until Mr. Blyleven showed up."

"What time was that?"

"Around one," he said. Then he frowned.

"What is it?"

"Well, like I told the federal investigators, that was a little unusual, Mr. Blyleven getting here so early. They weren't scheduled to take off until four-thirty. Even Larry didn't show up until three-thirty. He seemed surprised to see Blyleven."

"Did Blyleven explain why he'd arrived early?"

"Not to me. And really, it wasn't that big a deal."

"Did you talk to him at all?"

"Just to say hello. He asked if he could put his things on board."

"What things?"

"A flight bag and a briefcase."

"Is that all?"

"Yep."

"Nothing large enough to pack a parachute in?"

"Hell, no."

"Okay, so Blyleven put his flight bag and briefcase on the plane?"

"Yep."

"Did you go in with him?"

"No."

"So you didn't see where he put them?"

He shook his head. "I assume in one of the storage compartments."

"How long was he inside?"

"A few minutes, I guess."

"What did he do after that?"

"He walked over to the hangar door, sat on a folding chair, and waited for Larry."

"Wait a minute. You said he got here at one, and Foster didn't show up until three-thirty."

"Right."

"Blyleven just sat there for two and a half hours?"

"Yep."

"By himself?"

"Pretty much. I saw Chris talking to him for a few minutes."

"That would be Chris Esteves?"

"Right. Other than that, he didn't talk to anyone until Larry showed up at three-thirty. They spoke for a while, and then we rolled the plane out of the hangar so Larry could do his walk-around."

"Walk-around?"

"That's where the pilot checks all around the outside of the aircraft. When Larry was satisfied, he and Blyleven climbed on board and taxied away. That's the last I saw them."

"Did you actually see Blyleven get on the plane?"

"I did."

"You're positive it was him?"

"Hey, I was standing ten feet away."

"Was Chris Esteves there, too?"

"Yep."

"Where can I find him? No one around here seems to know him."

"You mean 'her.' She quit her job about four years ago, not long after the crash."

"*Because* of the crash?"

Doherty shook his head. "No, her husband bought a tavern, and she went to work with him."

"Where?"

"In Denver. A place called the Adobe Bar. Hey, look, I should be getting back to work."

"One more question. How did Blyleven seem to you that day? I mean, his mood."

"His mood? Excited."

"Oh?"

"He was always excited when he came here. He loved to fly."

4

I left the hangar, squinting, as if I'd just walked out of a movie matinee: *Dialogues with a Mechanic.*

I'd merely confirmed what I already knew, what Donald Warwick had told me. The aircraft had been checked out clean and empty the day prior to the crash, and it was guarded all night and watched all day. Then Foster and Blyleven and no one else got on and flew off into oblivion.

The only thing out of the ordinary was that Blyleven had arrived earlier than usual. So what? He'd put his carry-ons in the plane and then waited around for Foster. Did that mean he had a bomb in his flight bag? Maybe, maybe not. But he sure as hell wasn't hiding a body-double in his briefcase.

Still, something about it bothered me.

I opened my car door, but didn't get in, letting the heated air escape.

There were at least four more people I could talk to, three in Denver and one in Castle Rock. As I stood there trying to decide whether to drive north or south, something caught my eye.

A sign on a building.

I'd noticed it when I parked, but I hadn't thought much about it. The Perfect Landing Restaurant.

I crossed the parking lot and entered the building. There was a long counter and a lot of tables and chairs, all with a good view

19

of the runway through a wall of windows. It wasn't yet noon, so the place was practically empty, just a couple of beer drinkers who wore khaki pants, shirts with epaulets, huge-faced watches, and pearl-drop-shaped shades. Gee, do you suppose they're pilots?

I sat at the counter and ordered an iced tea from a hefty waitress wearing a yellow uniform and a friendly smile. Might as well have lunch. The day's special was tuna salad. I got a ham sandwich. You never know about tuna.

I swiveled in my seat and stared out the window. I could see several hangars to my right, although I wasn't sure which one I'd just been in. Whichever one it was, it was close by. Close enough for a guy to walk here and wait for his pilot to show up.

Blyleven had arrived two and a half hours before Foster, perhaps three full hours before he usually did. According to Doherty, he simply sat on a folding chair by the hangar door and waited. But why not wait in here, sit where it's comfortable, have a cup of coffee?

I asked the waitress, "How long has this restaurant been here?"

"Since they built the airport, I suppose."

"Longer than four years?"

"Honey, *I've* been here longer than four years."

"Is it open every day?"

"Twenty-four hours. You want some more iced tea?"

So why didn't Blyleven wait here? Why did he sit alone in a hangar smelling of machine oil for two and a half hours? Unless he wanted to make damn sure he was the first person to greet Foster. Again, why?

Maybe he wanted to tell Foster something before Foster saw the plane. Or climbed inside.

There was no way of knowing.

I ate my sandwich, paid the bill, and left a decent tip. Then I hit the road.

Castle Rock is about twenty miles south of Denver, a small town bisected by I-25, with the mountains on one side and rolling plains on the other. To most people in Denver, it's just a place you drive through on your way to Colorado Springs, or maybe Santa Fe. Of course, the residents of the town do not share this view. They place a lot of importance on each other's lives. So unlike city folk, who could give a damn about their neighbors, they tend to know everything about everybody in town. And they don't mind telling you—which is what I learned when I stopped to fill my tank at a self-service station.

The guy behind the cash register was as skinny as a POW with short hair and long sideburns. He was surrounded by packs of cigarettes and displays of scratch-and-win tickets. I asked him if he knew Earl Wilson.

"Sure do," he said. "Lives with his daughter Josie and her husband Phil. He's a general contractor, and a good one, too, if you know anyone who needs a house remodeled. That's Phil who's the contractor, not Earl."

"Right. Where do they live?"

He gave me directions and went on to say that Josie worked over at the bank, and their oldest boy, Jack, had just finished his freshman year at CSU (football scholarship, running back), and their other two kids were both in high school (the youngest one, Betty Anne, was smart as a whip—now that Henry, the middle child, was dumb, but he was more like his daddy, good with his hands), and they hadn't got another dog since their last one got hit by a hay truck, and he probably would have told me where they bought their shoes if I'd asked him.

"Tell Earl I said howdy."

"Sure thing."

Earl Wilson's neighborhood was quiet and shaded. The house was a two-story brick with a peaked roof, a covered front porch, and white-painted trim. A massive elm stood to one side, draping its shade across the tidy front lawn. As I went up the walk I could see thunderheads just starting to climb over the nearby hills to the west.

The man who answered the door was around sixty, wearing baggy blue slacks and a brown-and-white checkered short-sleeved shirt stretched tight across his pot belly. His nose was roughly the color of an eggplant, so I figured he was fond of a drink now and then. His glasses had clear plastic frames, and they slightly magnified his eyes. He gave me a suspicious look.

"Are you Earl Wilson?"

"That's right. Who're you?"

I could hear a ball game in the background. Not the Rockies—they played tonight. Here they were, past the All Star break and still looking for their thirty-fifth win. Hey, so what, they're only three years old.

I told him who I was. "I'd like to ask you a few questions."

"About what?" More suspicious than ever.

"Martin Blyleven."

A change came over him—brief, but it was there. Fear. He swallowed once and regained most of his composure. "What about him?"

"It's an insurance matter. Just a few details to clean up. Do you mind if I come in? Otherwise, you know, the neighbors . . ."

Wilson shot a glance past me. No one was out there, but he could imagine Old Mrs. Whosis wandering into her yard next door, turning an ear the size of a satellite dish this way.

"All right," he said hesitantly. "But just for a few minutes."

The living room had a fireplace in one wall that was ignored by the furniture—two blue wing chairs and an overstuffed sofa. They all had their attention directed toward the giant TV set in the corner. It was tuned to either TBS or WGN, because the Braves were playing the Cubs. Wilson picked up the tuner and killed the sound. The picture remained—a Cubbie taking a called third strike.

We sat in the wing chairs. Wilson crossed his legs and tried to look at ease. But he gripped the arms of the chair as if he were on a roller coaster.

"My granddaughter will be home soon," he said. "And when she gets here, you're leaving."

"No problem." I heard a sound like a furnace kicking on. Distant thunder.

"Besides," Wilson said, "I already told everything I know to the federal authorities back when it happened."

"Sure. How long did you work as a night watchman at Centennial Airport?"

"I was a security officer, not a fucking watchman."

"My error."

"Two and a half years."

"I'm just curious, what did you do before?"

"Don't give me 'just curious,' pal. I read you plain enough. If you want to know, I was a cop. Twenty-four years with the Englewood Police Department, before they forced me to retire."

"Forced you?"

He gave me a thin grin, released his grip on the chair, and turned his palms up. "I used to drink."

"I see. So then you went to work at Centennial?"

"That's right."

"And then you retired."

"Let's say they asked me to. Like I said, I used to drink. *Used to.* I haven't touched a drop in three years."

"Were you drinking the night before Blyleven's plane crashed?"

"I drank *every* night," he said, as if he were proud of it. Then he uncrossed his legs, leaned forward, and pointed a crooked finger at me. "But let me tell you something. Nothing got by me when I was on duty. Nothing went on out there unless I knew about it."

"Are you saying something went on out there that you knew about?"

He drew back. There was a loud roll of thunder. After it died away, he said, "I'm not saying anything like that."

"Of course not. How well did you know Martin Blyleven?"

He cleared his throat. "I knew who he was, that's all."

"Did you ever see him or talk to him away from the airport?"

"No," he said firmly.

"Tell me about that night before the crash."

"There's nothing to tell. I came on at eight that night and went off at eight the next morning. I checked the hangars and the office buildings like always."

"Did you enter any of the buildings?"

"No. Just checked outside doors and windows."

"Were you the only guard on duty?"

"The only one in that area, yeah."

"Did you see anyone?"

"Well, hell, yes. The airport is operational twenty-four hours, so there are always people around. Not many, though. And no one came anywhere *near* the hangar with Blyleven's plane," he said with emphasis.

"What kind of a person was Blyleven?"

He hesitated. "What do you mean?"

"I mean, in general. How would you describe him?"

He shrugged his shoulders, his hands gripping the chair's arms. "Just an average guy. Nothing special about him."

I felt he was holding back. I wished I had something to slap him with, knock him out of his defensive pose. Well, there was one thing.

"Can you keep a secret?"

He gave me an odd look. "What?"

"What if I told you that Martin Blyleven might not be dead."

"Wha—?"

His mouth dropped open and the color drained from his face.

"What would you think about that?"

"Impossible." His voice was a harsh whisper.

"Anything's possible," I told him.

"Are you saying he's *alive?*"

"I said 'what if.' "

Just then the front door burst open.

"Hi, Grandpa. I . . . Oh, sorry."

She was a pretty teenager in a brown-and-yellow fast food uniform and a matching cap. Her dark hair hung behind her in a long, single braid.

"That's all right, honey," Wilson said, rising. "This man was just leaving."

I stood and said, "We may need to talk again."

Wilson wanted to shout at me to get the hell out. But his granddaughter was watching. So he just ushered me to the door and held it open.

I nodded hello and good-bye to the young lady and walked out.

It was noticeably cooler outside than when I'd arrived. Black thunderheads now covered half the sky, obscuring the sun. I could feel Wilson's cold stare on my back as I went down the walk to my car. I stepped around to the driver's side and faced the house.

Wilson was still standing there, watching me. For a moment, I thought he might wave me back inside.

He shut the door.

5

I beat the rain out of town. As I sped north on the interstate I could see the sky behind me in my mirrors, black and roiling. It matched my thoughts about Earl Wilson.

He seemed ready to accept the possibility that Blyleven was alive. And that possibility scared the hell out of him. Why, I wondered. Obviously, he knew something he wasn't telling—about either Blyleven or the crash. And whatever it was, he hadn't told the federal authorities, I was certain of that.

I had a feeling that if I pushed the right buttons, Wilson would open up. What I needed was more information.

I found a pay phone outside a gas station at the southern end of the city and looked up the number for the Adobe Bar. The cool, stormy skies were far behind me now. The sun-cooked telephone was hot to the touch. The guy who answered told me that Chris Esteves wouldn't be there until six tonight.

That left me with most of the afternoon to kill.

Might as well go to church.

First, though, I needed to change my shirt. It was as limp as a tissue and semipitted out from my driving around all morning in the hot Olds. The old girl doesn't have air-conditioning—nor, for that matter, a telephone, a CD player, a wet bar, or a Jacuzzi—nor is she likely to in the near future. She's a 1956 aqua-and-white beauty, faithfully restored, and I intend to keep her that way. Respect for the elderly.

Although, a few months ago she got pretty well smashed up, and the guy who works on her suggested I sell her for parts and buy a new car. One with factory air. I considered it, but have you priced new cars lately? Forget about it. So I paid the repair bill and continued to sweat in the summer.

Back in the city I steered north on Lincoln Street, then east on Seventh Avenue to my apartment building—another gracefully aging lady.

A moving van was parked in front. Two burly young guys came down the ramp carrying a white leather love seat. I followed them up the walk.

"Be careful!" Mrs. Finch squawked at them from the front stoop. "I don't want you banging into my door frame!"

They mumbled and gave her nervous looks, a pair of draft horses being snapped at by a terrier.

And believe me, her bite matched her bark. We tenants walked carefully around her, knowing that eviction could be just a notion away in that batty brain of hers. I'm sure if she could afford to, she would live alone in the grand old house. After all, she'd been born here when it was a mansion, not an apartment building. Those were the days. Her father was a wealthy Denver merchant, and she and her mother and her sisters were all pretty and dressed in the height of fashion. I'd seen the yellowed, silver-framed photographs on her writing desk.

But now she was the last Finch, for she had never married. We tenants were necessary occupants—although not necessarily welcome. Sort of like stepchildren. And by God, we had better behave.

"Good afternoon, Mrs. Finch."

"Hmph, we'll see about that." She was intent on the men as they carried the love seat into the apartment across the hall from hers.

I'd been in the building something over three years, and during that time there had been a continuous stream of tenants through that particular apartment. Mrs. Finch lived right across the hall. She watched all of us closely, but she *scrutinized* the poor, unsuspecting souls who occupied "her" floor.

"I hope this one works out for you," I told her.

She pursed her lips and narrowed her eyes, which added a few hundred more wrinkles to her face. Her head barely reached the middle of my chest, but she had the uncanny ability to look down on me from there.

"Just what is that supposed to mean, mister?"

"Ah . . . nothing."

"And what are you doing home in the middle of the day?"

"I needed to change my—"

"You should be out looking for a job."

"I have a job, remember?"

She snorted. "I mean *decent* work. Not peeking through keyholes and nosing about in people's garbage."

She still lived in a time when keyholes were large enough to peek through. Although she wasn't far off about the garbage.

"Maybe something else will turn up," I said.

She gave me an impatient wave of the hand, then screeched at the two men, "Don't slide it, you fools, you'll scratch the floor!"

I climbed the stairs to the third story. There are two apartments on each floor—eight in all, counting the basement pair—and none of them are laid out the same way. You enter mine directly into the living room. Kitchen to the left, bedroom and bath straight on back.

I untied my tie, then peeled off my shirt and tossed it under the bathroom sink. My hamper. It was getting jammed up under there. Pretty soon I'd have to do my least favorite thing—sort the dry cleaning from the laundry and wash dirty clothes.

When I'd been married, Katherine and I divided the household chores. She took care of the laundry. It had been five years since she'd been murdered, and I still wasn't used to it.

Washing clothes, I mean.

I reapplied some twelve-hour underarm protection, then buttoned up a clean shirt (my next to last one), and walked through the living room and kitchen to the best part of the apartment— the balcony.

It faced east and so caught the afternoon shade. And it was high enough for a view over most of the nearby buildings and trees. On a clear day you could lean out and see Pike's Peak, seventy miles to the south. Of course, there was a much more alluring view closer at hand. Right across the alley, in fact. The upscale apartment over there had the only swimming pool in the neighborhood. And, as usual, several of the female tenants—flight attendants and those with night jobs—were working on their tans. To great effect, I might add.

I admired them for a while. Not that I'm a voyeur or a chauvinist pig. I can't even remember *why* I started leaving my binoculars out here.

When my arms got tired of holding them up, I tied my tie and turned my thoughts to holier ground.

6

The Church of the Nazarene was conveniently located near the Denver Country Club and the mansions that house much of the city's old money. Franklin Reed was nobody's fool. If you're going to gather a flock, the sheep might as well be financially sound. Reed's collection plate runneth over.

In fact, about twenty years ago it had run over a bit too much, causing something of a scandal. He had been indicted and found guilty of numerous counts of fraud—something to do with selling worthless penny stocks to the faithful members of his congregation. The court fined him heavily, forcing him to render unto Caesar. This he began doing the very next Sunday, tears in his eyes, begging forgiveness, pleading with his congregation to kick in a little extra to cover his fine. They did so with fervor—the very people he had fleeced in the first place.

Amen, brother.

The church itself looked like the prow of a mighty ship built of colored glass, shimmering in the hot sun. The roofline angled steeply upward and forward, peaking at the front corner of the edifice, a good four stories overhead. Nearby, there was parking for a thousand.

I turned off University Boulevard and guided the Olds a block or so along the sprawling, empty parking areas, then swung in behind the church. It wasn't quite as impressive from the rear—a long, single-story stretch of offices and classrooms. There were little brass plates set into the brick beside a half-dozen or so blond-wood doors. I found one marked simply, *Pastor Franklin Reed.*

I wondered if pastors were like barbers and took Mondays off. I folded my sunglasses into my jacket pocket and went inside.

The office was cool and softly lit. On the wall to my left was a painting of Jesus, praying, sad face lifted toward heaven. As if to remind Him of what lay ahead, the opposing wall was adorned with a large brass machine-tooled cross.

"May I help you, sir?"

"I'd like to speak to Pastor Reed."

"Do you have an appointment?"

She was a stern-looking, middle-aged woman wearing a suit coat over a blouse with a Puritan collar. The pastor's first line of defense. Behind her, a computer screen winked knowingly. Was I the only person who didn't own one of those damn things?

"No, I don't have an appointment, but—"

"Pastor Reed is extremely busy," she said, as if only an idiot or an atheist wouldn't know that. "Perhaps I can help you."

"Perhaps you can. I'm here about a dead man."

That got her attention. I showed her some identification and told her I was investigating the death of Martin Blyleven.

She hesitated, then picked up the phone, keeping her eyes on mine. She punched a button and said, "There's a private detective here asking for Pastor Reed. . . . No, sir, it has to do with Martin Blyleven. . . . Yes, sir." She hung up. "If you'll just have a seat."

I sat under the portrait of Jesus, which left me staring at the cross on the opposite wall. At least it wasn't a crucifix. I'd seen plenty of those in my parochial-school days. Catholics weren't content with metaphor. They wanted to see the Actual Guy up there, nailed in place, blood dripping from wounds, the more detail, the better. And he was always sculpted with the body of a long-distance runner, long and lean with well-defined muscles, wearing a diaper, on display for everyone to see. You always felt a little uncomfortable looking at him. Maybe that was the idea.

A man came through an adjoining door and glanced at the receptionist, who glanced at me. He wasn't Reed, whom I had seen

on TV. But he was wearing an expensive suit, so maybe I was
getting closer.

"I'm Matthew Styles," he said, without offering to shake
hands. "May I help you?"

He was about ten years my senior, forty-five to fifty, and
roughly my size—six feet or a little more, about one ninety. He
had a broad forehead and a lot of hair, carefully moussed into
place. He wore designer eyeglasses that probably turned dark when
he went outside. There was a wedding band on his ring finger and
a heavy gold watch on his wrist. He smiled, but it was empty. A
con man.

I introduced myself and gave him my own con job, the Canadian insurance company and so forth. I saw the wheels turning in
his head: *Do I shut the door in this clown's face and maybe have
to deal with him later, or do I get it over with now?*

He made up his mind and said, "I'm afraid Pastor Reed is
unavailable. But I'd be happy to answer your questions. This
way, please."

Styles led me out of the reception area and down a hallway
past several closed doors. His was the next to the last.

"Please sit down," he said, putting his desk between us. There
were a few papers on the blotter, which he immediately removed
and shoved in a drawer. On one end of the desk sat—what else?—
a computer. The walls were unadorned, except for a simple
wooden cross and a framed certificate with a gold seal.

"I assume you've already spoken to the authorities about this,"
he said.

"The insurance people have."

"By the way, which insurance company are you working for?"

"Fidelity Life of Ontario," I said off the top of my head.
"What they're looking for now—what I'm looking for—are details of a more personal nature."

"Such as?"

I took out my notebook and pen. "How long did Martin Blyleven work for the church?"

"Not quite two years."

"Were you here when he was hired?"

Styles smiled his fake smile. "I've been Pastor Reed's chief assistant for many years. Yes, I was here. In fact, I'm the one who hired Martin. And it had nothing to do with nepotism. He was a good accountant.''

"Nepotism?"

"He was married to my sister."

"Vivian Armis?"

"Yes."

Well, well. Although he didn't sound too happy about it.

I asked, "Were you and Blyleven friends before their marriage?"

"I met Martin when they were engaged. After they were married, I offered him the job."

"Was this a new position?"

"No. Our previous accountant was retiring."

"Name?"

Styles frowned. "Is that important?"

"Probably not. I'm just trying to be thorough. You know how these insurance companies are." I looked at him with wide-eyed expectancy and held my pen poised above my pad.

He gave me a sour look and said, "Bill McPhee."

"Phone number? Address?"

"It's probably in our records. Somewhere."

"Right. Tell me, how often did Blyleven fly to Tucson?"

"About once a month."

"For what purpose?"

"Church business."

"Can you be more specific?"

He shot his wrist and looked pointedly at his eight-thousand-dollar watch. "I can for the next four minutes, at which time I'm due in a meeting with Pastor Reed." He folded his hands on the desk. "Briefly, the church manages an organization called World Flock, which builds hospitals and orphanages overseas for those less fortunate than ourselves."

"Those who tell time by the sun."

"Excuse me?"

"Did Blyleven work directly for World Flock?"

Styles was scowling, still working on telling time by the sun. He said, "He kept the accounts."

"Why did he fly there to do it? I thought everything was done with those." I nodded toward the plastic-and-glass cube on the end of his desk.

"Computers have their limitations," he said.

I got the feeling there was more to it than that. "How long would he stay in Tucson?"

"He'd fly down one day and come back the next."

"Always on the church-owned plane?"

"Yes, of course."

"Wouldn't it have been cheaper to book a seat on a commercial airline?"

He turned his head slightly and aimed one eye at me. "What exactly is your point?"

"Did Blyleven ever fly the plane himself?"

"No, of course not. He wasn't qualified. Lawrence Foster was the pilot."

"Was Foster a full-time employee?"

"No. We kept him on a small retainer and then paid him for each trip."

"Is the set-up the same now?"

Styles flinched. "I beg your pardon?"

"Do you have an accountant and a pilot who make the monthly trip to Tucson?"

He glanced at his watch, then stood. "I'm sorry, your time is up."

As if I were a contestant on *Jeopardy*. I stood and said, "No problem. I can come back tomorrow."

"No. That wouldn't—"

"Or the day after."

He sighed heavily and said, "Two more minutes, that's it." He remained standing.

"Does your present accountant fly to Tucson?"

"No. Now we have someone there who keeps track of things for World Flock. I make the flight occasionally to oversee the operation."

" 'Occasionally' being . . . ?"

"Monthly. In fact, I'm flying there Saturday. You have one minute."

"Who do you think blew up the plane?"

"I have no idea."

"Blyleven?"

"That's absurd. He had no reason."

"Was he depressed?"

"Not at all."

"Could he have been killed by an enemy?"

"As far as I know, he had no enemies."

"What about Foster?"

"I wouldn't know."

"Could it have been done by an enemy of your church? Or of Franklin Reed?"

Styles gave me a superior look. "Pastor Reed doesn't make enemies, Mr. Lomax. He saves souls." He came around his desk. "Now I really must insist that you leave."

As he ushered me toward the door, I said offhandedly, "Anyone ever wonder if Blyleven might be alive?"

"For a time we. . . ." He caught himself. "Of course not."

"For a time you what?"

"Good-bye, Mr. Lomax."

"Sure. Thanks for your help."

I started down the hallway. From behind me I heard, "We're waiting, Matthew."

I looked back and saw Franklin Reed standing in an open doorway at the end of the hall. He was dressed in angelic white. Curly gray hair framed his head like a halo. He glanced at me and spoke in a low voice.

"Who is that?"

Matthew Styles said something I couldn't hear. He nudged Reed into the room. The door closed behind them.

Now that they'd gotten the pagan out of the way, they could get on with God's work.

7

I sat in my car and tried to finish the sentence that Matthew Styles had begun.

"For a time we . . ." Believed that Martin Blyleven was alive.

"For a time we . . ." Considered it a possibility.

Something along those lines, I was sure. But why would they even consider it? Everything pointed toward Blyleven's death. That is, everything known by the feds and the insurance companies. Maybe Styles and Reed knew something else.

And if Blyleven *hadn't* died in that crash, then he'd probably murdered two people—his stand-in and Lawrence Foster.

I wondered if there was anything in Blyleven's past that indicated violence. Like a criminal record.

I knew a few Denver cops who would have that information at the tips of their computer-tapping fingers. That is, if they felt they owed me enough of a favor to put forth the effort. Which, at the moment, none of them did. There were other ways I could get what I wanted, but all of them took time and legwork. I prefer one-stop shopping.

I drove to my office through rush-hour traffic and flipped through the Rolodex until I found the number I wanted.

"Agent Cochran's office."

"May I speak to him, please? This is Jacob Lomax."

"One moment."

35

Michael Cochran was the special agent in charge in the FBI's Denver office. I'd worked with him a few months ago at the tail end of a case I'd been on. Actually, "worked" was too strong a word. I merely answered every question he asked and handed him all the information I had about a start-up drug operation. An uncle and a nephew named Dykstra were manufacturing a designer drug called "ice" and shipping it interstate under cover of a legitimate business. It was the legitimate business that I'd been concerned with, not the drugs. But I'd found myself in the middle of things. Namely, the drug lab blew up and I shot one of the Dykstras. The feds, Cochran in particular, had several hundred questions for me. I'd helped them as much as I could, and Cochran had seemed grateful. But grateful enough to do me a favor?

"Hello, Mr. Lomax. This is Agent Cochran."

Agent Cochran. Not Michael. Definitely not Mike. Apparently, I was speaking with a federal employee, not a good buddy.

"I'm sure you're not in the habit of doing favors for private investigators," I said.

"That is absolutely correct."

"But I have one to ask. A small one."

He said nothing. Then again, he didn't hang up.

"I'm working on an insurance case," I said. "I need to know if one of the principals has a criminal record. And if so, I need details."

"Requests of that kind can only be granted to the police or appropriate government agencies." As though he were reading it from a pamphlet.

"I understand. As I said, I'm asking for a favor."

He was silent, thinking it over. "This is not standard procedure, you understand."

"Yes, I do."

He was silent again, recalling, I hoped, all the work I had saved him with the Dykstras.

Finally, he sighed. "Name?"

"Martin Blyleven." I flipped through my notes. "Middle initial, E." I also gave him Blyleven's social security number. I didn't

tell him, though, that Blyleven was presumed dead. Why compli-
cate things?

But he said, "Blyleven. Why does that name sound familiar?"
And I knew he'd check it out.

"He died in a plane crash four years ago."

"I remember now. We assisted in that investigation." He
paused. "And you want to know if this dead man had a criminal record?"

"Yes."

"Why?"

I hate lying to someone who's about to grant me a favor. Which
doesn't mean I won't. I said, "There's a dispute about a rider on
one of the old policies."

He cursed under his breath. Insurance companies, I think. Or
maybe PIs. "I suppose I owe you something from that Dykstra
business."

"Well . . ."

"But in the future," he added, "any requests must be made
through official channels."

"Sure thing."

"I'll get back to you." He hung up.

I checked my watch. Five-thirty. Still too early to catch Chris
Esteves at the Adobe Bar. I looked up Nora Foster in the phone
book. Too easy, there was only one. Of course, she might not be
the one I wanted. For all I knew, my Nora could have remarried
and moved to Bosnia or Bolivia or worse, the Bronx.

She answered on the third ring.

After I introduced myself, I asked if she was the widow of
Lawrence Foster.

"Yes," she said matter-of-factly. No catch in her throat, no hint
of sorrow in her voice. But then, the man had been dead for
four years.

"I'm working for a Canadian insurance company," I said,
spewing out the same lie that I'd used all day. Only this time I felt
guilty about it. Because she was a widow? Possibly. But maybe I
felt a bond with her. Our spouses both had suffered violent deaths.
"I'd like to come over and ask you some questions."

"When?" she asked.

"Whenever it's convenient for you."
A pause. "I suppose it would be all right."
It was my turn to ask, "When?"
"Now."

8

Nora Foster lived in a modest brick home on South Fillmore Street, not too far from the University of Denver. The street dead-ended perpendicular to a long, narrow park, a few houses down from hers. I could see some kids over there tossing a Frisbee, and an old guy walking his dog on a leash. I parked in the shade of a grandfatherly willow and went up the uneven stone walk.

The lawn had just been mowed. There were clippings on the stones, and I could smell the fresh-cut grass. It smelled good. I stood on the porch and rang the bell. More nice smells—a box bordered the entire porch, overflowing with a riot of flowers.

Nora Foster answered the door.

I introduced myself, and she let me in.

She was an attractive woman in her early thirties with startling green eyes and long auburn hair that fell smoothly to her shoulders. She wore faded blue jeans and a sleeveless white blouse. She had an even tan.

I followed her through the house. The living room was comfortably furnished, the dining area was cramped, and the kitchen was long and narrow and had a tile floor.

"I thought we could sit outside," she said, glancing back at me, tossing her hair. "It's finally starting to cool off."

The deck in back was shaded by an immense sycamore tree with leaves the size of saucers. There was a round redwood table surrounded by four chairs with puffy blue-and-white cushions. She motioned me toward one, and I settled into it.

"Would you like something to drink?"

"What are you having?"

"A beer."

"Sounds good."

She went back inside, leaving me alone in the backyard. Again, I smelled freshly-mown grass, which always made me somewhat nostalgic—summers as a kid, no school, baseball, bike riding, playing fetch with my dog and a slobbery tennis ball. I noticed a water bowl near the back door, and there were small, dead patches of grass. Nora Foster owned a dog. A detective's mind never rests.

Nora came out with two silver cans of Coors and two glasses and set them on the table.

"Thanks."

She sat down, not across the table, but ninety degrees away from me. She tipped her glass and poured beer carefully down the side. I did the same, just to be polite. A faint breeze stirred the air and brought with it the sweet scent of flowers. Or perhaps it was Nora Foster. I reminded myself why I was there.

"I appreciate your helping me," I said. "I know it must be difficult for you to talk about . . . the accident."

She sipped her beer and shook her head. "Not anymore." But her eyes briefly lost their focus. Then she crinkled her brow and gave me a half-smile. "I'm not sure, though, how much help I can be."

"How long did your husband work for Franklin Reed's church?"

"About two years."

The same as Martin Blyleven. "What did he do before that? I mean, what sort of work?"

She smiled. "He flew. Every chance he got. It was his great passion in life. Crop-dusters, trainers, whatever kind of work he could find. He owned his own plane, too, an old Piper, and he hired it out whenever he could."

"For what?"

She sipped her beer, then ran her fingertip around the rim of the glass. "Just about anything. He toted banners over football games and parades. He took photographers up for aerial views of snowy peaks and sunsets. Anyone who could pay, he'd take them up." She grinned. "Sometimes he'd give them more than they'd paid for."

"What do you mean?"

"I'll give you a perfect example. Larry and I met through a mutual friend, and our first date was—what else?—a plane ride. He flew me all around the city and the foothills, and then he started showing off, doing barrel loops, stalls, and so on. Scared the hell out of me. He thought I was having great fun, and I was just trying not to puke." She grinned crookedly and shook her head. "When we got back to the airport my knees were so wobbly I could hardly stand up. I chewed him out, called him a maniac, and told him I never wanted to see him again. Of course, six months later we were married." Her grin had softened into a smile. "He was persistent, I'll say that for him." She sipped her beer.

"How long were you married?"

"Seven years. Brian was six when Larry was killed."

"That must have been tough on both of you."

She nodded. "More so on Brian, I think. He loved his dad. And, of course, financially it was a strain. There was little insurance money, and I was earning barely enough to support us. I sold Larry's plane to help us get by."

She stared wistfully across the yard. There was a wooden privacy fence, but we were sitting high enough to see over it into the next yard. Her gaze, though, went miles beyond that.

"Being a single parent is not what it's made out to be on TV sitcoms," she said, still staring in the distance. "I don't know if it's fair to Brian."

She kept looking over the fence, as if the answer to her problem lay there. I drank my beer and waited for her to return.

She did. "Sorry."

"That's all right. Tell me about Larry's job with the church."

"What do you want to know?"

"How did he get it?"

"As I recall, someone at Centennial Airport told him the church was looking for a pilot. He was interviewed by Pastor Reed's assistant. His name escapes me."

"Matthew Styles?"

"That's it."

"What exactly was the arrangement?"

"Larry was on retainer, a thousand dollars a month. When he flew, they paid him another thousand plus food and lodging. This was a sweet deal for Larry—two thousand a month for two days work, and he had lots of free time to hustle up other jobs."

"That seems like a lot for them to pay."

"I suppose. Larry didn't question it, though. Of course, he had to be ready to fly whenever they called."

"How much advance notice did they give?"

"No more than two days. Usually only one."

"Was it always the same time of month?"

"Not exactly. Every three to five weeks."

Styles had told me that Blyleven flew to Tucson to do the accounting books for World Flock. I assumed it had been on a regular basis, either at the beginning or the end of every month. Obviously, this wasn't the case.

"Did they fly anywhere besides Tucson?"

"No."

"Your husband would've told you if they had, wouldn't he?"

"Yes, of course."

"Did they ever land anywhere between here and Tucson?"

She frowned, crinkling her brow. "No. Why would they?"

"I don't know. Did your husband ever take anyone besides Martin Blyleven?"

"I think the first few times, Matthew Styles went along. But after that, it was just Larry and Blyleven."

"They stayed overnight, right?"

"Yes."

"Where?"

Nora Foster cocked her head and gave me a quirky smile. "Well, that was a little odd. Larry stayed in a hotel near the airport, but Blyleven stayed at a condo owned by the church. At least, that's what he told Larry. All Larry knew for sure was that someone would pick up Blyleven at the airport. In a big stretch, he said."

"A limo?"

She nodded and swirled the last half of her beer in her glass, building foam. "And it wasn't a church limo, either."

"No?"

She shook her head. "Blyleven told Larry that the church didn't own any limousines."

"So it wasn't church people who picked him up?"

"I guess not." she said.

"Who was it?"

"I don't know. Neither did Larry. He said Blyleven never talked about what went on down there, except that it was 'church business.' "

"I see. Did Blyleven return to the airport in the limo?"

"I believe so. I know that Larry would meet him there in the morning and they'd fly home."

"Did Blyleven ever carry anything down there or back?"

"Like what?"

"Packages, boxes, whatever."

"No. Nothing besides an overnight bag. They each brought one of those. And Blyleven had a briefcase."

She started to sip her beer, but then stopped and set the glass down. "There was something about that briefcase, though. Larry mentioned it."

"What?"

She frowned, thinking, then shook her head. "I can't recall what it was."

"Was there something unusual about it?"

"I'm trying to remember."

"What sort of a briefcase?"

"Just an ordinary one, I guess. I never saw it. I think Larry said it was leather."

I heard noises inside the house, and a moment later a dog and a boy came out the back door. The boy was around ten, and he wore jeans with a ripped knee and a black-and-purple Rockies T-shirt. He gave me a suspicious look. I wondered if there were lots of strange men who came calling on his mother. Somehow, I doubted it.

He turned from me and said, "When are we gonna eat, Mom?"

"Pretty soon, honey."

Meanwhile, his dog had become fascinated with my pants' cuffs.

"Lady, stop that," Nora said. Then, "Brian, this is Mr. Lomax. He's a private investigator." As if that would impress him. It didn't.

"It's nice to meet you," I said. I nodded at his shirt. "I see you're a Rockies fan."

"I guess. Mom, I'm going in." And he did. I never was too swell with kids. Lady, however, plopped down at my side and let me scratch behind her ears.

Nora Foster shrugged an apology. "Brian's not very friendly toward strangers."

"That's probably a healthy attitude. Look, I won't keep you from your dinner. I just want to know, did you ever meet Martin Blyleven?"

"No."

"What did your husband tell you about him?"

She pressed her lips together and looked up at the leafy tent overhead. "Nothing that really stands out. He was just an average sort of guy, I guess. Although Larry called him 'anal.' "

I had to smile at that. "Why?"

"Picky about little things, I guess."

"I see." No doubt a prerequisite for an accountant. "Anything else?"

She shook her head. "No."

"Well, I appreciate your help." I handed her my card. "If you remember anything about Blyleven's briefcase, would you call me?"

"Yes."

When she took the card, our fingers touched. No electric current passed between us, but if she had asked me to stay for dinner, I would have. She didn't.

She led me through the house. Lady trailed behind us.

Brian was in the living room playing a video game on the TV set. He didn't turn around.

Nora stood at the door, saying good-bye.

I drove off, feeling something stirring in my gut. A tiny blue flame. I wanted to know who had killed Larry Foster, whether it was Martin Blyleven during the act of suicide or someone else committing murder. I'd never met Foster, but I had the feeling I would have liked him. I hated that he was dead.

More than that, I hated that Nora was without her husband and Brian was without his dad.

9

___

Colfax and Wadsworth are two heavily traveled commercial streets that intersect west of the city. The continuous flow of traffic has painted a grimy mixture of road dust and carbon monoxide on all the storefronts in the area.

The Adobe Bar was no exception.

It was a single-story, flat-roofed box, once white, now dull gray, its windows painted to keep out bright lights and Peeping Toms. Not that anyone ever *walked* around here. There was barely room for a dirty strip of sidewalk to squeeze between the building and the stream of cars and trucks.

I turned into the parking lot, a cracked asphalt apron that wrapped around three sides of the building. City-tough weeds pushed up around the edges. I parked the Olds between a battered GMC pickup truck and a ten-year-old Camaro with no wheel covers and went inside.

It was smoky and loud.

There was a bar running down the right-hand wall fronted by a dozen stools, most of them occupied, mostly by men—blue-collar workers, if they worked at all. To the left were tables and booths, also filled. There was a pool table near the back wall where two guys were laughing and shouting and banging around the balls. Except for a few geezers sucking back draws and shots in a corner booth, I was the oldest customer in the place.

I sat at the bar between a skinny young woman with long brown hair and a laugh that rattled the fillings in my molars and a guy the size of a Volkswagen wearing a Harley-Davidson T-shirt.

The bartender needed another arm. She held a pitcher under a tap with one hand, pulled three beer bottles out of the cooler with the other, rang up a sale on the register, shoved some change at the only waitress, loaded up one tray, and emptied another. On her way over to me she dipped a couple of glasses into a soapy basin, then a rinse basin, then set them on a rubber drain mat at the end of the bar.

"What can I get you?"

She was forty or so, and she wore a man's oversize black-and-white striped shirt, like a referee's, with the baggy short sleeves rolled up past her elbows. She wiped the bar in front of me, emptied the ashtray, and laid down a cocktail napkin that immediately soaked up moisture on the bar.

"A Bud."

She was back in a flash with my beer, then snatched up my five and brought back the change before I even had a chance to say thanks.

The Harley man next to me rumbled, "Give us another round, Chris."

If she was Chris Esteves, she wasn't going to be free for an in-depth conversation, at least for a while.

So I sat there and drank beer and watched the game. The TV was on a shelf near the ceiling behind the bar. No sound, but a good picture, Reynoso was throwing against the Cards, top of the first, two outs, nobody on.

By the seventh inning they were tied at three, and I was on my fourth beer. The bar had quieted down. There were empty stools on both sides of me, and only a few tables were occupied. The waitress was sitting at the far end of the bar smoking a cigarette and talking to a Hispanic guy wearing an LA Raiders cap. Chris Esteves was talking seriously to a big guy with a black ponytail. Earlier, I'd seen him busing tables, helping Chris out behind the bar, and getting between the two pool players, who had looked about ready to fight. I thought at first he might be her husband. But after I saw the way she ordered him around, I figured he was

the part-time helper and full-time bouncer. Of course, he still
might be her husband.

I watched her take some bills out of the till and count them
carefully into his hand, talking all the time. He nodded, shoved
the money in his pocket, and walked out.

Then she came down to my end of the bar.

"Another Bud?"

"No, I'm fine, thanks. You're Chris Esteves, right?"

"That's me." She had frizzy black hair and a strong face, with
high cheekbones and a prominent chin. There were laugh lines at
the corners of her large, brown eyes, and her eyebrows were thin,
painted arcs.

"Thomas Doherty said I could find you here."

"God, I haven't seen him in a couple of years. How's he doing?
Still at Centennial?"

"Yes. In fact, I was out there this morning talking to him about
Martin Blyleven."

"Oh?" A frown wrinkled her forehead. "Wait a minute, are
you a cop?"

She'd said "cop" loud enough to alert anyone in the bar who
might be dodging warrants or holding grass. A few heads turned
our way.

"Far from it," I told her. I gave her my card. "I'm working
for an insurance company, trying to find out what I can about
Blyleven's death."

"I already told those fucking feds all I know."

"This isn't a federal thing. I just want to ask—"

"Bull*shit*!" This came from the pool table, the same two characters who had been arguing earlier. The only difference now was
they were drunker. "I don't give a *fuck*! It touched the *eight first*!"

Chris ignored them and said, "How do I know for sure *you're*
not a fed?"

I made an "X" on my chest. "Cross my heart and hope to
die?"

I think she started to smile. But she was interrupted by a crash
of chairs. The two pool shooters were wrestling each other to the
floor. She said, "Assholes," and ran down the length of the bar

and out the other end shouting, *"Break it up, goddamn it, that's enough!"*

The two guys were back on their feet. But they hadn't had enough. In fact, they were just getting started, wrestling and punching, bouncing fists off shoulders and ears and noggins. Everyone in the bar—a handful of guys and a couple of women—was standing, but nobody seemed eager to interfere. In fact, most of them were enjoying the show.

Chris was shouting at the two men to stop. Then she grabbed the nearest guy by his shirt and tugged. Which put her too close to the action. A flying elbow caught her in the upper chest and sent her stumbling backward onto the floor.

Well, shit, Lomax to the rescue.

I hustled over there, pushing aside a few enthralled onlookers. I lifted a cue stick from the table, said, "Fight's over, gentlemen," and smacked the elbow-thrower across the back of the head with the butt end. He fell into the arms of his opponent, then dropped to his knees. The other guy, a moon-faced character with a beer keg for a stomach, shoved his partner aside, called me a motherfucker, and reached toward the table for a pool ball. I brought the cue stick down on the back of his hand, and that was the end of that.

"God *damn*," he said, clutching his hand and glaring at me with tears in his eyes.

Chris was on her feet now. She gave the guy a shove.

"Get out of here, Neal, you're eighty-sixed."

"He started it." He nodded toward his pal on the floor, who was moaning and holding his head. There was some blood, but not much.

"Both of you," Chris said. "Find someplace else to do your fighting."

"But—"

"GET OUT!"

They did, Neal trying to help his buddy along and cradle his wounded hand at the same time. Chris followed them to the door, and I followed her. Everyone else sat down. She turned from the open doorway, bumping into me. I was still watching the two guys, because now was when things could get deadly. There are more guns than gloves in glove compartments.

"Where's the key that locks this door?"

"The key? I've got it. Why?"

I watched Neal and friend climb into a battered Chevy S-10. They drove away.

"No reason," I said. I handed her the cue stick. "I should practice more."

She smiled, then winced, rubbing her chest above her breasts. "Let me buy you a beer."

We went back to the bar and I sat in my stool. The bouncer with the ponytail walked in carrying two sacks of burgers.

Chris said, "You missed all the action," and told him what had happened.

"I should've tossed those two fuckers out before I left," he said, barely glancing at me. I thought he might come over and thank me, but he actually looked angry, as if I were horning in on his job. He took one of the sacks to a table and began eating by himself.

Chris brought over a Bud for me and a draw for herself. She took a small bag of fries from the sack and set them on the bar between us.

"Help yourself."

I ate a couple of fries and wiped the grease off on the bar napkin.

Chris said, "Why is the insurance company still asking questions about that plane crash? I thought they would have settled everything by now."

"Different company," I told her, starting to feel stupid using the same old lie. "How well did you know Martin Blyleven?"

"Not well at all. I'd see him at the airport now and then."

"What about Lawrence Foster?"

"Larry?" she smiled. "Sure, I knew him. Everybody around there did. He was a great guy." Her smile faded and she shook her head. "That was the shitty part, that he died."

"Do you know anyone that would have wanted to kill him?"

"Christ, no. He'd give you the shirt off his back if you asked him. I doubt he had an enemy in the world."

"Did he ever seem depressed to you?"

"Do you mean could he have committed suicide by blowing up the plane? No way. He was a happy-go-lucky guy. Plus, he loved his wife and kid. He'd *never* leave them like that." She shook her head again. "They're the ones I really feel sorry for."

"Thomas Doherty said you were there when Blyleven and Foster took off that day."

She nodded, unwrapping her burger. "I hope you don't mind. This is my dinner."

"Go ahead." Although the smell was making my stomach rumble. "You saw them get on the plane?"

"Mm, hm." She chewed a bite of burger.

"You're sure it was Blyleven? Not just somebody who might have looked like him?"

She nodded, still chewing. Then she washed it down with a swig of beer and said, "I was standing right next to him. The feds asked me the same thing. About a thousand times, the assholes." She took a ferocious bite of burger.

I let her finish chewing it. "What have you got against the feds? If you don't mind my asking."

She gave me a long, cynical look, still trying to see if there was a cop hidden somewhere inside. Then she took a swig of beer and said, "Because they fucked over my little brother, that's why." She picked up a fry, stared at it for a moment, then put it down. "Well, okay, it was partly his fault. He got busted with some coke, not much, a quarter ounce. They could have charged him with possession, first offense, given him probation and community service—you know? Like they do for *rich* people." She sighed. "But they wanted to make an example out of him. Or maybe they just didn't like his attitude, because he refused to rat on the people he bought it from. So they hung a distribution charge on him, and he got ten to fifteen years in a fucking federal prison. He'll be out next year." She stared down at her burger. "But he changed in there. He's harder. It's like he's ... not my brother anymore." She looked up at me. "*That's* why I hate the goddamn feds. After the crash, they asked me all sorts of questions. Sure, it was a terrible tragedy, but I told them as little as possible. Fuck 'em." She pushed her burger aside and gulped down some beer.

"Did you withhold information?"

"No," she snapped. Then her look softened. "Well, not exactly. I mean, those arrogant bastards paraded through there like they owned the place, demanding to know every little detail about me and my job and Foster and Blyleven. I finally got sick of it—of *them*—so I just gave them yes and no answers."

"What did you leave out?"

She gave me a brief, suspicious look. "Nothing important."

"But something."

She hesitated. "They asked me if I'd talked to Foster that morning. I told them sure, and then spent the next *two hours* going over every little detail of the conversation, which hadn't amounted to shit. So when they asked me if I'd talked to Blyleven, I said no. I lied, so what."

"So you did talk to him."

"Briefly."

"What about?"

"An earthquake in Mexico City. I heard about it on the radio that morning when I drove to the airport. I was concerned because my husband has relatives there. I mentioned it to Blyleven. He got very upset."

"What do you mean?"

"I mean, his jaw dropped and his face turned white and he started pumping me for details about what I'd heard. I thought maybe he had friends or family down there, too."

"Did he?"

"I asked him, and he said no." She shrugged. "That's it. But you know what?"

"What?"

"It felt good lying to the feds, even for something that small. The assholes."

10

The next morning, I phoned Roger Armis at home. I wanted to catch him before he left for work. Actually, it was Vivian who I wanted to speak with. I hoped that by now Armis had told her about my involvement. I didn't want to proceed further until I had the answers to one or two dozen questions, starting with, Why would Blyleven be upset about an earthquake in Mexico City?

Armis's line was busy.

While I waited for it to clear, I could deal with a more crucial matter. My laundry. I was down to my last clean pair of jockey shorts.

I dug out an old sea bag and began stuffing it with clothes from under the bathroom sink. I yanked the drawstrings, but the bag was too full to close. I dragged it into the living room and reached for the phone. It rang before I picked it up.

Agent Cochran.

"Thanks for calling back," I said.

"I was going to leave a message on your office machine, then I thought I'd try to catch you at home. I have the information you requested. That is, the lack of it."

"Excuse me?"

"Martin E. Blyleven has no arrest record."

"Oh."

"However, his prints are on file at Quantico. A copy was faxed here this morning."

"Why was Blyleven printed?"

"He was in the Army. I'll send you what I have. What's your number?"

"My address is—"

"Your fax number."

"Oh? I've been meaning to get one of those."

He heaved a bureaucratic sigh. "I'll put it in the mail."

"I'd appreciate it."

After I hung up, I phoned Armis again. Still busy.

Shit. No way out of it now. I slung the bag over my shoulder and tromped down three flights of stairs to the basement of the grand old house.

It's a bit creepy down there—weak lighting, squeaky linoleum floors, sickly yellow plaster walls. There's a short hallway with four white wooden doors, each sprouting a brass filigreed door-knob. They open, respectively, into a small apartment (vacant); an immense combination furnace room and storage area (including a solid cedar closet, where Mrs. Finch's mother no doubt hung her fur coats in the summer); another small apartment (old George the handyman); and the laundry room.

Actually, it's more than a laundry room, but all Mrs. Finch allows us to use are the washer and dryer. At the far end there's a locked cabinet and a work table equipped with a vise and a circular saw— the province of old George. One long wall is filled with shelves, mostly empty. By this fall, though, they'd be loaded with Mrs. Finch's preserves: beets, pickles, peaches, and raspberry jam.

I heaved my bag onto the counter beside the washer and began pulling out dirty clothes, dark things in one pile, light things in another.

One good thing about this type of work is that it frees your mind. . . .

I discounted the idea that the midair explosion had to do with Lawrence Foster. Everyone liked him and he led a happy life. Besides, it was Blyleven who supposedly had returned from the grave, not Foster. And it was Blyleven who was beginning to look suspicious: arriving very early at the airport, being met in Tucson by a non-church-owned limo, and fretting about an earthquake in Mexico City.

I could see two sets of premises. One, Blyleven was alive or he was dead. And two, Blyleven put the bomb on the plane or somebody else did. Put these together and you get four possibilities. I looked at each one.

First, Blyleven was dead and he brought the bomb on the plane.

In a word, suicide. For whatever reason. Although, I've always believed there was only one reason why people take their own lives. Depression. They've lost their jobs or their loved ones or their health or their self-respect, and life seems worse than whatever might follow, if anything. On the other hand, maybe Blyleven brought the bomb on the plane for some other reason, and it went off accidentally. Yeah, sure, he always goes to Tucson with his toothbrush and his C-4 explosives. Not likely. And I also doubted suicide. Blyleven was happy and healthy with a good job and a nice family. Why kill himself?

The second possibility was that Blyleven was dead and someone else put the bomb on the plane.

Murder. This seemed impossible, for one very good reason. According to the FBI, the bomb had gone off right in Blyleven's face. How could a murderer get him to cooperate? Give him a package with a card: Do Not Open Until Take-off? Besides, Blyleven didn't bring any packages on board. Just a small flight bag and a briefcase.

The third possibility was that Blyleven was alive and he had put the bomb on the plane.

On the face of it, this was the most suspicious scenario. Not only to me, but to the FBI, Donald Warwick, and Pioneer Insurance. Martin Blyleven had faked his own death, possibly so his wife and child could collect four hundred thousand dollars. And perhaps so he could return four years later and claim it. Although this sounded farfetched.

And of course, once you looked into this theory, you had problems. How did Blyleven get off the plane and get somebody to take his place? How did he get Foster to cooperate? Because certainly nothing could be done on that small plane without the knowledge and participation of the pilot. And assuming Blyleven *could* smuggle someone on board, how the hell could he get him to hold a bomb in his lap and set it off? And do it while Foster was calmly flying the plane. And bail out without a parachute. Hard to believe.

So was the fourth and last possibility, that Blyleven was alive and someone else put the bomb on the plane. Same problems. How do you get Blyleven off the plane, and someone else on, then blow up the plane—all under the eye, if not the approval of the pilot? And who was the stand-in? Warwick said he and the FBI had done thorough background checks on Foster and Blyleven and had found nothing suspicious, no close friends or associates who'd suddenly disappeared.

So I had four possibilities and all of them were impossible.

Except, perhaps, the first. Blyleven had brought the bomb on board and committed suicide, never mind why.

Then who was the man trying to blackmail Roger and Vivian Armis? And more, how could he so thoroughly convince Vivian that he was Blyleven, back from the dead?

All I could do was guess. In fact, that's all I'd been doing since—

I heard voices.

". . . laundry room to your right and . . . well, this door is *supposed* to be closed."

A young woman entered the laundry room just ahead of Mrs. Finch. She was a knockout, and I don't mean Finch. Late twenties, I'd guess, wearing yellow shorts and a tank top that was filled to capacity. She was tanned the color of creamed coffee, and her blond hair fell to her shoulders. Cascaded, actually.

She gave me an open smile and said, "Hi."

"Hello there," I said, as cool and nonchalant as could be. Holding an armload of damp laundry. I tossed it in the dryer. "Please tell me you're the new tenant."

She laughed. What a great laugh. Or maybe I'd been spending too much time alone.

"I'm Sharon Hoffman," she said.

"Jake Lomax. Pleased to meet you." I waved a hand at the concrete walls and empty shelves. "This is my place, and welcome to it."

She smiled. A terrific smile. "Do you do everyone's laundry?"

"We could probably work something out."

"You're *supposed* to keep that door closed," Mrs. Finch spat, taking the shine off my brilliant repartee.

I should explain that Mrs. Finch does not appreciate tenants of the opposite sex getting too chummy with one another. She considers it scandalous. Perhaps even incestuous. After all, this is her house and she is the matron and we are all her, well, stepchildren. Which can be a real pain in the ass. I stay, though, because the rent is cheap, the location great, and you never knew who might move in across the hall from her.

"How many times do I have to tell you to keep that door closed, Mr. Lomax?"

"Eleven?"

Another great smile from Sharon Hoffman.

"That is not funny."

"Sorry," I said.

Mrs. Finch snorted at me, then turned her attention to Sharon Hoffman, laying down a few rules. The washer and dryer could be used any day except Monday, no earlier than eight in the morning and no later than nine at night, and they both must be left absolutely *clean.* (A quick, hard look my way.) The shelves are not to be used. George's worktable and tools are not to be used. And above all, the door is to be closed *at all times.* (A *long,* hard look my way.) She ushered Sharon toward the door.

Sharon turned and said, "I'll be seeing you."

"I look forward to it."

Mrs. Finch asked her to wait in the hall, and then she scuttled toward me, stopping in the center of the room. She skewered the air with a gnarly finger and said, "I'll talk to *you* later."

Gulp.

She turned on her heel and bustled out, eager to tell Sharon what a despicable scoundrel I was and Lord knew why she continued to let me live under her roof.

I spent the next two hours washing and drying and folding. Then I carefully packed my bag, made *certain* that the door was closed, and trudged up the three flights of stairs to my apartment.

I unlocked the door and stepped inside.

Something hard and heavy smacked me in the head.

11

It's funny how your mind sometimes works. My first thought was that Mrs. Finch had finally gone over the edge and decided to beat the crap out of me.

No such luck.

I slumped forward into the arms of a bear of a man, who held me away from him with one hand and drove his fist into my stomach. I dropped to my knees, feebly grabbing at him.

He rumbled, "One more, Jack" to someone behind me.

I took another smack on the head. Lights out.

When I came to I was sitting in one of my kitchen chairs, face down on the table. My skull felt as if it had been cracked open like an egg, spilling my gray-matter yolk down the side of my face. I hoped it was only blood. My arms hung down between my legs, and my wrists were bound together with what felt like tape. I didn't move or open my eyes. Someone was sitting near me at the table—I could hear him breathing—and at least two other guys were searching my apartment. Their voices carried from the bedroom.

Guy One: "Look in all the pockets, jackets and pants."

Guy Two: "I know what I'm doing."

Guy One: "Then act like it."

Guy Two: "Hey, there's a safe in the back of the closet."

Guy One: "Wait a minute." Sounds of movement. "Locked. Go see if he's awake yet."

Footsteps, then Guy Two, clearer now, probably standing in the doorway: "Wedge, Manny wants to know if he's awake."

Wedge said, "I'll just check." He sounded like the bear-man who had punched me in the stomach. Now he grabbed my ear and twisted. It hurt like hell.

I moaned.

"He's coming around."

Guy Two, his voice somewhat muffled: "He's awake, Manny."

Sounds of approaching footsteps.

Manny said, "Sit him up."

Hands grabbed my shoulders and pulled me back in the chair. I moaned again, for effect. Also because the sudden movement made my head feel as if part of it were still lying on the table. I blinked my eyes against the light.

The bear-man named Wedge was sitting at the table with me, as if he'd just dropped by for coffee. He wore a billowy Hawaiian shirt with red and yellow flowers and enough fabric to pitch a tent. His close-cropped black beard was flecked with gray, and it framed rosy cheeks and a round, red nose. Just like Santa. Except Santa didn't have scars and calcium deposits on his knuckles. He laid his beefy, hairy forearms on the table, folded his thick hands, gave me a sad smile, and said, "How was your nap?"

"Peaceful."

"You hear that, Manny? Peaceful."

Manny looked down on me from a few feet away. He was an oily-looking character with smooth olive skin and black hair moussed back and tied in a little tail. He wore a dark-green silk shirt buttoned at the neck and the cuffs, gray slacks, and black alligator slippers. His lips were curved into a cupid's bow, sensitive, almost feminine. His eyes, though, were hooded and cold. Snake's eyes.

I didn't believe for a minute that these characters were burglars here to crack my safe. Nor did I think they were friends of the two brawlers I'd cue-sticked last night at the Adobe Bar. If they'd come here just to beat me up, they would have done it by now and been gone.

This was something more serious. And it didn't take long to find out what.

The guy standing behind me said, "Where's Martin Blyleven?"

"Who?"

He tapped me on top of the head with something small and hard. Given the present condition of my noggin, it felt like he'd used an engine block. Purely out of reflex, I spun out of the chair to get my hands on the son of a bitch. My ankles were taped together. I nearly fell down. Wedge grabbed a fistful of my shirt and shoved me back in the chair.

At least I'd gotten a look at the head-banger. He was short and stocky with brown hair cut close on the sides and wavy on top. He wore a black polo shirt and shit-eating grin. There was a tiny diamond in his left earlobe.

"First things first," Manny said. He looked down on me with cold, expressionless eyes. "What's the combination to the safe?"

"There's nothing in there you'd want, believe me."

"The combination."

"It's not even my safe. It was here when I moved in and I've never had it open."

"Jack?"

An explosion in my head. I slumped forward, nearly blacking out, just getting my bound hands up in time to keep from flattening my nose on the table.

Manny spoke from half a mile away. "Not so hard, Jack. He's no good to us if his brains are scrambled."

Hands pulled me upright in the chair. My head was roaring and my vision was blurred. I blinked my eyes, finally focusing them on Wedge, still seated across from me, still wearing a sad smile.

Manny said, "I'm not sure how much of this you can take, Jake." Jake. As if we were old pals. "There's always the chance of brain damage. You should probably just give me the combination."

I gave it to him.

"Watch him," Manny said, and left the room.

The only things I kept in the safe were my two handguns, about two thousand dollars in mad money, and the title to my Olds. It didn't take long for Manny to find that out and return to my side.

"I was hoping I'd find something useful in there, so I wouldn't have to rely on your word. But now I have to ask you. Where is Martin Blyleven?''

"Marvin who?''

Manny smiled, without so much as putting a crease in his smooth, oily skin. "Martin," he said. "Blyleven."

"Oh, him. He's dead."

"Don't lie to us," Wedge rumbled. "You *know* he's alive because you told—''

"Wedge, please," Manny said. Then he looked at me. "We can make this hard or easy, it's up to you. Where's Blyleven?''

"Crown Hill Cemetery. That is, the pieces of him they found in a desert in Arizona.''

"Wait," he said quickly, holding up his hand. Not to me, but to Jack. "Don't hit him. I want him conscious. There are other ways to do this." He glanced down at me and curled up one corner of his mouth. "More unpleasant ways, I'm afraid." He turned his back on me and started pulling open kitchen drawers. The third one he got to held the silverware. And the knives. He rummaged around inside.

"Listen," I said, "Blyleven's dead. Everybody knows that. The feds, the insurance companies, they'll all tell you the same thing.''

"But you seem to believe he's alive," Manny said. He came back to the table and set down a knife, just out of my reach. It was a paring knife with a stubby wooden handle and a short, very sharp blade.

"No," I said, "I don't believe that at all. I was hired by a Canadian insurance company to look into the circumstances of his death. Do you understand? Death. As in dead.''

But Manny didn't seem to be listening to me. He was going through the cupboards, actually humming to himself, as if he were searching for the ingredients to bake me a cake.

"Ah, here we are.''

He came back to the table with a small cardboard box of toothpicks—the good kind, tapered at the ends and thick and square in the middle. Nothing but the best in the Lomax kitchen. Manny selected one and held it up, as if he were a jeweler examining a stone. Then he picked up the knife.

"You've been asking a lot of questions about Blyleven, as if—"

"For the insurance company."

"—as if you're trying to *find* him." He started shaving one end of the toothpick with the knife.

I'm ashamed to say that I was tempted to tell him to go ask Vivian Armis, let her and her husband deal with this. Besides, she knew more about Blyleven than I did. Of course, she might be reluctant to talk, and there was no telling what Manny and Wedge and Jack would do to her to change her mind.

"I told you, he's six feet under."

Manny blew on the end of the toothpick. "Yes, that's what you've told us." He tested the point with the tip of his finger. "But now you're going to tell us the truth. Wedge?"

Wedge reached for me.

And with nothing to lose, I launched myself backward out of the chair, knocking it over, twisting as I did so, reaching for Jack's throat. Of course, it would have been more effective if my wrists and ankles hadn't been wrapped in duct tape. As it was, I got Jack by the shoulder. He stumbled back in surprise, pulling free, and I fell to the floor, where I could do little more than flop around like a hooked fish. Wedge straddled me and drove his fist into my kidney. Then he dragged me gasping back to the table.

He kicked aside the chair, lifted me to my knees, and pulled my arms straight out across the table. He put his hands across my forearms and leaned his considerable weight on them, pinning me there. Just to make certain I wasn't going anywhere, Jack crouched behind me and wrapped his arms around my head and neck in a figure-four hold.

"Don't choke him," Manny said calmly. "I want him awake."

"Don't worry."

Manny tucked his prized toothpick behind his ear, then reached for my hands. I bunched them in fists, suspecting what was coming. But he managed to pry loose the little finger on my left hand. He bent it back, not trying to break it, just holding it there, separating it from the others. Then he retrieved his needle-pointed toothpick.

"I'll ask you again. Where is Martin Blyleven?"

"As far as I know he's dead. I—"

Pain flamed through my hand, up my arm, and across my chest.

All Manny had done was jam the toothpick under my fingernail halfway to the cuticle. It felt as if he'd shoved in an ice pick all the way to the handle. I tried to jerk away, but Wedge held me firmly in place. And I couldn't even cry out because Jack had me in a stranglehold. I breathed heavily through clenched teeth. The pain slowly ebbed, pooling in my wrist and hand.

Manny still held my little finger in his fist, but he'd let go of the toothpick. It stuck out from under my nail like the bowsprit of a model ship.

"Such a small thing," Manny said with no expression, "yet so much pain. Now, please. Where's Martin Blyleven?"

"I told you," I said, my voice half strangled. "Crown Hill Cem—"

Manny slammed the toothpick with the palm of his hand. Fire seared through my arm and chest, and my brain seemed to be filled with a bright white light. The light slowly faded and the room came back into view: Manny on one side of the table, Wedge on the other. The toothpick was still under my nail, deeper than before. My hand and arm throbbed.

"It gets worse," Manny said, "trust me. And just when you think you've reached your limit, I start on the next finger. Why put yourself through that? Just tell me where—"

A sharp rapping on the front door.

Manny, Wedge, and I all looked that way. I assume Jack did, too. He tightened his arm under my chin to keep me from yelling for help. Nobody made a sound. I was praying that Vaz, whose apartment was just below mine, had heard what was going on and called the cops. With any luck they were out there now, guns drawn.

Another sharp rap and then a squawking voice: "All right, Mr. Lomax, open up. I know you're in there."

Mrs. Finch to the rescue.

12

Manny put his face close to mine and whispered, "Who is that?"

Jack eased his chokehold enough for me to croak, "My landlady."

More rapping, short and sharp. "I have a few things to say to you, Mr. Lomax," Mrs. Finch squawked. "And I don't intend to do it through a closed door. Now, either you open up or I will."

"She means it," I told Manny. "She has a key."

"All right, mister," Finch said.

A key scratched in the lock.

Manny said, "Wedge."

The big man let go of my arms and moved quickly and quietly around the counter that divided the kitchen area from the living room. He stood at the far side of the front door, meaty hands hanging loosely at his sides.

"Don't hurt—"

Jack tightened his chokehold on me.

The locked clicked and the door swung open. Mrs. Finch entered talking: "Now I heard you in here before, Mr. Lomax, so don't try to pretend that you're—"

Wedge clamped a hand over her mouth and chin, holding her without effort. With his free hand he pulled the bunch of keys from the lock and closed the door. Mrs. Finch did not struggle, whether from shock or the certain knowledge of futility, I wasn't certain. Her eyes were wide behind her glasses.

"This is no good," Manny said.

"It'll get worse." My voice was a harsh whisper.

Manny waved a hand at Jack, who eased the pressure around my throat.

"Meaning what?"

"Her husband will come up here next. And before long the rest of the nosy tenants will be milling around out there. That's a couple dozen witnesses to deal with." Actually, Mrs. Finch had been a widow for twenty years and there were only six other people in the building, most of whom minded their own business. But it sounded worse my way. Manny thought so, too, I could tell by the look on his face.

"Now what?" Jack said.

"We could snuff this old bird and take him with us," Wedge offered.

"Oh, that would be smart," I said. "The three of you carrying a bound man out of the building and down the street in broad daylight. Where did you get these guys, Manny?"

"Shut up."

"Now what?" Jack still wanted to know.

Manny pursed his lips, making up his mind. "Let's get the fuck out of here."

"And do what with him?"

"Nothing." Manny gave me a cold smile. "For now."

He got the roll of duct tape from the kitchen counter, tore off a strip, and plastered it over my mouth. Jack pulled me backward and threw me to the floor. I tried not to hit my hand, because Manny's customized toothpick was still stuck under my fingernail. But just the movement brought enough pain to make my eyes water. I blinked away the tears and watched Jack and Wedge bind Mrs. Finch's hands and feet and tape her mouth. They left her on the couch. Wedge tossed the bunch of keys beside her, then followed Manny and Jack out the door. I heard them clumping down the stairs.

I pried the tape off my mouth, straining to keep my little finger and the toothpick away from my face. Then I pointed my hands toward me as if I were praying, carefully clamped my teeth on the toothpick, and yanked it out.

I lay there for a few minutes as the waves of pain subsided in my arm and hand. I pushed myself to my feet. The knife Manny had used was lying on the table. I picked it up, wondering if it might be easier to cut Mrs. Finch's bonds than my own.

Then I heard heavy footfalls coming up the stairs.

Had Manny changed his mind?

Quickly, I squatted down and cut through the tape that bound my ankles. I hustled toward the door, trying to cut the tape from my wrists. Not enough time. I held the knife in both fists, keeping it at waist level, ready to thrust up and out at the first person who crashed through the door.

A knock.

"Jacob, are you in there?"

I relaxed. "Come on in, Vaz."

Vassily Botvinnov opened the door. He's a barrel-chested man in his sixties, with a ruddy face, eyebrows like gerbils, and spindly legs draped in baggy brown slacks. Despite the heat, he wore a long-sleeved flannel shirt. He took one step into the apartment, then froze, eyes bulging under heavy, hairy brows. Why not? Mrs. Finch lay bound and gagged on the couch and I was holding a knife.

"Jacob?"

"It's a long story. You want to cut off this tape?"

After Vaz freed me, I went to Mrs. Finch and carefully lifted the tape from her mouth.

"I won't *have* this rough-and-tumble behavior in my house," she said at once. "Do you and your friends think this is some sort of *gymnasium* that they can come in and wrestle around? Here, here, I'll do that." She slapped away my hands and unwound the tape from her hose-supported ankles. I wasn't sure whether she was in shock or simply loonier than I'd thought. She stood up and briskly smoothed her dress, glaring at me. "And another thing, I won't have you fraternizing with my new tenant. You stay away from her, is that clear?"

"Yes, ma'am." I handed her the loaded ring of keys.

She snatched them from me, stomped out, and slammed the door behind her.

Vaz looked more confused than ever. "Those three were *friends* of yours?"

"Hardly."

"When I heard them on the stairs, I looked out and saw them hurrying by. They didn't look very amiable. Who are they?"

"Let me call the cops first. And take some aspirin." My head was booming.

While we waited for the police to arrive, I told Vaz about the three visitors, my present case, and Martin Blyleven. Then I suggested that there was no sense in his getting involved in this. He left, reluctantly.

I checked the safe. The door hung open. My two handguns were still there, and so was the envelope that had once held my cash. Just the envelope, no cash. Now, any cheap punk worth his swagger would have taken the guns, too. Jack and Wedge would have, if only to sell. The .357 magnum was worth a few hundred bucks easy.

But Manny had left them behind. He had all the guns he needed. A pro.

A pair of uniforms showed up forty minutes later.

The elder of the two, a tough-looking veteran, asked all the questions. She filled out her report with a ballpoint pen, while the radio on her belt chattered in muted tones. Her partner, a baby-faced Hispanic walked around the apartment looking at everything, touching nothing.

I told her what had happened, leaving out only a few nonessential details—like Blyleven and Vaz and Mrs. Finch (why bother the dear old bird any further?). However, I did volunteer to go through the police mug books. In fact, I insisted.

"A detective will contact you," the female cop said. Then she squinted at me, her eyes narrowing on either side of her slightly crooked nose. "Lomax. That name's familiar. Didn't you used to be a Denver cop?"

"Right."

"When did you retire?"

Christ, did I look that old? "I didn't retire, I quit. About five years ago."

She pursed her lips and nodded. "Yeah, well, it's not for everyone."

After they left, I phoned Roger Armis at the bank where he worked. The receptionist put me on hold. I passed the time by examining my little finger. It still hurt like hell, clear up to the wrist. There was a thin, bloodred line under the nail from the end to the cuticle. That was it. Not even any blood. What had Manny said? *Such a small thing, yet so much pain.* I hoped I got the chance to further explore that theory with him.

Armis came on the line, and I told him we needed to talk.

"Have you learned something about Blyleven?"

"Not over the phone," I said. "And I need to speak with your wife, too."

"I . . . I haven't yet told her about you."

"Well, call her and tell her now. We need to meet today."

He was silent for a moment. I could almost hear him chewing the inside of his cheek. Finally, he said, "All right. I usually go home at noon."

"I'll be there."

"Please wait until one."

"Fine." Hey, why spoil their lunch?

13

Roger and Vivian Armis lived in a substantial two-story brick-and-frame house at the end of a cul-de-sac a few blocks off South Kipling Street in Lakewood. I saw a lot of kids in the neighborhood—riding bikes in the hot sun, playing kids' games, staring at the ancient Oldsmobile cruising down their street. I wondered if one of them was little Chelsea Armis.

I parked in the wide concrete driveway. Armis must have seen me through the picture window, because he opened the door before I rang the bell.

He looked distressed—more so than he'd sounded on the phone. Something was up.

"Come in," he said, avoiding my eyes.

The living room was cool and sterile. Like a lot of houses in suburbia, the "front room" was rarely used, and the furniture was pretty much for show. If the family members weren't eating in the kitchen or sleeping upstairs in the bedrooms, they were probably in the rec room, recreating—that is, watching TV.

I sat on an expensive-looking chair with cherry-wood legs and hard cushions. Armis perched on the edge of the couch. It was upholstered in a tasteful floral pattern and looked brand new. Beside Armis was a small, round end table, unencumbered except for a photograph in a fancy frame. The Armis family. Little five-year-old Chelsea wore a frilly yellow dress and stood between her mother and her adoptive father, reaching up to hold their hands. Vivian and Roger were dressed conservatively, perhaps for church—she in a peach-colored outfit, and he in a blue suit and tie.

Armis put his hands on his knees and frowned at them. He cleared his throat. "I, ah, explained to Vivian that I had hired you, and, well, she became upset, and ah . . ."

"Where is your wife?"

"She's upstairs. She, that is, we, we've decided that we no longer need your services."

"Oh?"

"Yes. We're going to pay the money to Martin."

"And hope he simply goes away."

"Well . . . yes."

"You don't even know for certain that it's Blyleven."

"Vivian is certain."

"So you've said. But when I spoke to you on the phone less than two hours ago, you were anxious to hear what I'd found out about him. Now you don't seem to care."

"It doesn't matter what you've found."

"And why, all of a sudden?"

He wouldn't look me in the eye. "Really, this no longer concerns you."

"The hell it doesn't."

He blinked at me. "Excuse me?"

"This morning I was bounced around my apartment by three ugly characters looking for Blyleven. Manny, Jack, and Wedge. Those names mean anything to you?"

He shook his head. "No, I . . . They were looking for *Martin?*"

"And it wasn't to fill out a foursome for golf. Now look, so far I haven't told the police about—"

"The police?" His face lost its color.

"I told them about the attack, but not about Blyleven or you. That could change, though, unless I get some answers. I think it's time I spoke to your wife."

"I . . . I don't know if—"

"It's all right, Roger."

Vivian Armis entered the room. I hadn't heard any movement

preceding her appearance, so I figured she'd been standing just outside the doorway, listening.

She was a handsome woman, around thirty, with an oval face, wide-set brown eyes, and chestnut hair curled beneath her chin. She wore a straw-colored summer dress and little make-up. Roger Armis looked much older beside her, more like a father than a husband.

"Please sit down," she told us both.

She took a seat beside her husband, who seemed more fretful than she. She gave his hand a squeeze, then folded her hands in her lap. Her nails were long and squared off, shiny with clear polish.

"What did these three men want with Martin?" she asked me without preamble. Obviously, she had been eavesdropping, and she wasn't apologizing for it.

"I don't know," I said. "But I'd say they meant him harm. Who are they?"

"I have no idea, Mr. Lomax. And I'm sorry to have involved you in this. If I had told Roger everything in the beginning, he would have never hired you. He would have known that Martin is alive."

"Maybe you should tell *me* everything."

"You don't have to say a word, Vivian," Armis said quickly.

She nodded, her eyes on me. "Yes, I think I do."

She began by explaining that seven years ago, when she was barely out of college, she'd met Martin Blyleven, and after a brief courtship they were married. Almost immediately, Vivian's brother, Matthew Styles, got Martin a job as an accountant for Franklin Reed's Church of the Nazarene. A year later, Vivian gave birth to Chelsea. And six months after that, Martin Blyleven learned that he had inoperable cancer.

"He said he'd been to several doctors," Vivian said. "They'd all told him the same thing—he had only a few months to live."

Blyleven couldn't face spending his last months waiting in agony as the cancer ate him alive. He decided to take his own life. Vivian was horrified. She begged him to reconsider. But he was adamant. In fact, he was more concerned with Vivian and

Chelsea's welfare than with his own. If he committed suicide, his life insurance would be voided. They had few assets. In effect, he would be leaving his family destitute. Unless he could make his death look like an accident.

"I was completely against it," Vivian said. She paused. "At first, anyway. But I had to face the fact that Chelsea and I would be left alone. And, I'm sorry to say, I began to see the logic of it."

"Did you also see that it was criminal fraud?"

"Now just a minute," Armis said, defending his wife.

She gave his hand a squeeze and nodded tightly at me. "Yes, of course I did. That's why I told no one about this, not even Roger. Until today."

Blyleven told Vivian that he had a foolproof plan and that he'd enlisted the aid of the church's pilot, Lawrence Foster. One evening Foster came to the house. Martin introduced him to Vivian and said that he and Foster were going for a long drive, that they would be gone for a few days, and that Vivian was to phone the church the next day and say that Martin was sick with the flu. She was to tell no one that Foster had been there or that Martin and Foster had gone away together.

"Where did they go?"

"Martin wouldn't tell me. He said the less I knew, the better."

"You said they were going on a long drive. Are you sure they didn't fly? Foster had his own plane."

She shook her head. "No, they drove. When Martin came back two nights later, he was . . . wrinkled, road-weary. And the car was splattered with bugs, as if it had been a long time on the highway. Martin even left early for work the next morning so he could take it to a car wash."

"You said 'Martin came back.' Was Foster with him?"

"No."

"Didn't Foster leave his car here while they were gone?"

"No. They took both cars."

"On a two-day road trip? Are you sure?"

She frowned, and bit her lower lip. "That's how I remember it. I'm trying to think why I do."

Armis and I waited.

Vivian's head came up, her brown eyes wide. "Road food," she said. "Martin had me pack two sacks. Some celery, a couple of apples, and a few candy bars in each. And two bottles of Evian from the fridge. They each took a sack and a bottle with them in their cars when they left."

"And you have no idea where they went."

"No." She swallowed with difficulty and looked away. "Less than a week later the plane . . . blew up. Martin had killed himself. Or so I believed. But he'd also killed Foster. If I had known what he'd been planning, I . . ." She shook her head, blinking rapidly to keep away the tears. Maybe she was thinking about Foster's widow and child. I was.

She said, "I tried to convince myself that *Foster* had blown up the plane. And, who knows? Maybe he did."

I seriously doubted that. "Had you and Martin ever been to Mexico City?" I was thinking about his final conversation with Chris Esteves.

"What?" She sniffed once and sat up a little straighter, regaining her composure. "No."

"Did either of you have friends or relatives there?"

"No. But why—"

"Did Martin ever mention Mexico City to you in any context?"

She frowned and shook her head. "No, not that I recall."

"So you wouldn't know why an earthquake down there would greatly upset him."

"Well . . . no. An earthquake?"

If Blyleven had planned to hide out in Mexico, he hadn't told Vivian. "Prior to the crash, did Martin do anything out of the ordinary? I mean, aside from his two-day road trip with Foster."

She hesitated. "Yes. The night before. Of course, at the time I didn't know it was 'the night before.' He left the house late, around eleven. I was getting ready for bed. He said he'd be gone for a few hours and for me not to tell anyone."

"Where did he go?"

"I don't know."

"Was Foster with him?"

"No. At least, he didn't come to the house."

"You didn't tell any of this to the police or the insurance company or the federal investigators, did you?"

"No, I . . . I was afraid."

"Afraid you wouldn't collect Martin's life insurance?"

"Now just a damn minute," Armis said. "You have no right to—"

"It's all right, Roger," Vivian said.

He closed his mouth and blew air through his nose.

"Yes," she said to me. "The money was a consideration. After all, Martin was gone, and Chelsea and I were alone. But mostly I was afraid that the police would implicate me in what Martin had done. That is, what I *thought* he had done. Suicide . . . and murder. I was terrified they would put me in jail, or at the very least, take Chelsea away. So I lied. By omission. I told them nothing about Martin's cancer or his two-day trip or his absence the night before the crash. And now he . . . threatens to tell."

"You mean, someone who claims to be him."

"It's him."

"But how could it be? The plane crash aside, he had inoperable cancer. He should be dead."

Vivian shook her head. Her face looked pinched. "He didn't have cancer. Some months after the crash I spoke to our family doctor. He said that Martin had been in perfect health."

"I see. So why would he put a bomb on the plane?"

"He *didn't*," she said loudly. "He *swore* to me when he phoned. Martin is no murderer. He said someone else blew up the plane."

"Who?"

"The man who died with Foster."

"What's his name?"

"Martin . . . wouldn't tell me."

"Did he say *why* the plane was blown up?"

"No," she said quietly.

"Or why he disappeared?"

"No."

"Or where he's been for four years?"

"No. All I know is that he's back."

"But you haven't actually seen him."

She shook her head. "I've only spoken to him on the phone."

"Are you sure it's his voice?"

"His voice is . . . different. A harsh whisper. He said he had an accident that permanently damaged his larynx."

"Oh, that's convenient."

"I know, I refused to believe him, too. And it wasn't only his voice that was different. It was his attitude. He seemed cold. Mean. I knew he couldn't be Martin."

"What changed your mind?"

"He . . . called me 'Kitten.' "

"Kitten."

Armis shifted in his seat. He looked embarrassed. Vivian didn't.

"It was a name we used . . . in bed. I was his kitten and he was my tiger. It was our secret. We never told anyone."

"How can you be sure *he* didn't?"

"It wasn't only that, Mr. Lomax. I questioned him—not at length, because he said he couldn't stay on the phone for long. But he knew almost everything I asked him."

"Almost?"

"Look," she said defensively, "we were together for less than two years, and we've been apart for four. Memories get cloudy." She sighed. "Besides, there was one thing he knew in great detail. The events prior to the crash. And only three people knew about that—Martin, myself, and Lawrence Foster. And Foster's body was positively identified. It *has* to be Martin who called."

"Maybe he told someone else those things," I said. "Perhaps inadvertently. A golf partner or a drinking buddy."

"Martin rarely drank, certainly not in bars. And he didn't play golf or any other sport. Unless you consider chess a sport."

"Who did he play chess with?"

"No one in particular. He belonged to the Denver chess club. They met once a week. Tuesdays, I think."

"Did he go every week?"

"Yes. Right up until he . . . disappeared."

"Did he ever mention anyone's name from the club?"

"Not that I recall," she said with some impatience. "And really, Mr. Lomax, what does it matter? Martin has returned, and unless we pay him four hundred thousand dollars, he'll . . . ruin our lives.''

She looked sick. And it wasn't because of the money. The man she once had been married to, and had loved, had viciously turned against her. Or so it seemed.

"I think we should call his bluff,'' I said.

They stared at me as if I were slobbering.

"If this man is Martin,'' I explained, ''he couldn't possibly come forward. He can't implicate you without implicating himself. The feds will land on him with both feet. In fact, you could cooperate with them, testify, and—''

Vivian was shaking her head no.

"He doesn't intend to show himself,'' she said. ''He can prove to the authorities—anonymously, of course—that I lied during their investigation. I could be charged with obstructing justice, if not conspiracy to commit murder. So you see? We have to pay.''

"Maybe not,'' I said. ''We still have time to find a way out of this.''

"Less than a week,'' Armis said. ''Martin said he'd call Monday and for us to have the money ready.''

Vivian nodded in agreement. ''There's no other way.''

"There are always other ways. Let me keep looking into this. When we have more of the picture, we might see a solution. Right now there's too much we don't know. For instance, why would Martin want everyone to think he was dead?''

Vivian raised her eyebrows. ''Well . . . I suppose for the money. The four hundred thousand.''

"If that were true, he wouldn't have waited four years. The money could be gone. In fact, it *is* gone, isn't it?''

"Well . . . yes.''

"So why would he want to fake his death?''

Vivian slowly shook her head. ''I have no idea.''

I had three without even trying. Manny, Jack, and Wedge.

Before I left, I asked Vivian if I could borrow a photo of Blyleven. She gave me the same one I'd seen in Donald Warwick's office, a three-by-five color shot from the chest up. Same triangular face and pointed chin, same narrow nose and wide-set eyes. Same smile.

Although now it seemed different.

Pained.

14

I drove to the Denver Police Building on Thirteenth Street to admire their collection of photographs.

Notwithstanding Vivian Armis's conviction that Martin Blyleven was alive, I still wasn't certain. The scales seemed balanced.

On the *dead* side was the preponderance of circumstantial evidence, the result of an exhaustive investigation by federal, state, and private cops: Blyleven got on the plane, the plane blew up, pieces of his body were found, and no one had seen him since. On the *alive* side was the blackmailer. True, thus far he was merely a voice on the telephone, but he seemed to know things that only Blyleven could know.

And then there was Blyleven's mysterious two-day road trip. Did that indicate he was preparing for his death or preparing to *fake* his death?

And what about the blackmail artist? If he was a fraud, someone pretending to be Blyleven, how could he know so much? And why did he wait until now to come forward? On the other side, if it really was Blyleven, then why did he wait four years to resurrect himself?

Dead or alive? The scales were flat even.

One thing seemed certain. If it really was Blyleven, then to pull a stunt like this, to return in this way, he had to be desperate.

Or insane.

The only sure way to get all the answers was to find the man and ask him. For the moment, that was impossible. I still had a few trails left to follow, though. One beckoned more than the others. Or perhaps it was merely my aching head and throbbing little finger.

The detective assigned to my assault was named Flannery, a beefy redhead with freckles on his face and the back of his hands. I described my assailants to him and answered his questions. Well, most of them. He sat me at a table at the edge of the busy squad room, plunked down a stack of mug books, and left me alone.

For most of the afternoon I flipped pages and scanned photographs. After a while they started to blur together, until it seemed as if there were only four men in those books, pictured over and over again: a White, a Black, a Hispanic, and an Asian.

I was looking primarily for Manny, the leader of the trio. I didn't find him. Nor did I find the bear-man called Wedge. But I did come across a front and profile of one Jonathan Granger.

His friends called him Jack. I still had lumps on my head from his sap.

I waved Detective Flannery over and said, "This one looks kind of familiar. What do you have on him?"

Flannery pulled up Jack's file on his computer screen.

"Oh, he's a real sweetheart," Flannery said.

Jack had a long list of arrests and half a dozen convictions, dating back to his teenage years in Wyoming. Most of it was strong-arm stuff: extortion, assault, assault with a deadly weapon. He'd done thirty-two months in Canon City for manslaughter.

I wasn't as concerned with his resumé, though, as with his whereabouts. His last known address was on West Twenty-fifth Avenue, just off Federal Boulevard.

"You know," I said to Flannery, tapping the photo in the mug book with my sore hand, "I'm not so sure, after all."

"We could bring him in for a line-up, see how he looks in person."

"That won't be necessary."

He turned from the monitor and gave me a tired look. "Meaning what?"

"I don't think it's him. I'm sorry."

He squinted. "Don't bullshit me. He's one of your assailants, isn't he?"

I said nothing.

"You're not planning a little personal revenge, I hope."

"Me?"

He reached over, took my sport coat by the lapel, and lifted it away from my side. "Have you got a carry permit for that?"

It seemed prudent to start packing the .38. I showed him the permit.

He made a face and shook his head. "A private dick."

"Right."

"Yeah, well, you'd better not get it caught in a wringer. Because if I find out you've been taking the law in your own hands, I'll jump down your throat far enough to kick out your liver. Calling yourself a private eye doesn't mean squat."

"Don't I know it."

He gave me an impatient wave and said, "Get the fuck out of my sight."

I drove to the last known address of Jonathan "Jack" Granger. It was in an area of north Denver that had once been Italian, but now was Hispanic. Many of the blocks in this part of town were poor, but well tended—pride in one's home having nothing to do with money. Of course, there are slobs in every economic bracket.

Take Jack, for instance.

His address was one end of a triplex, the units arranged side by side, facing the street with sagging wooden porches, broken and taped windows, and a yard that hadn't seen a lawn in decades.

There was a low-slung Chevy convertible, top and windows down, parked in the lengthening shade at the east end of the triplex. Four young Hispanics sat inside, their heads wrapped in blue bandannas, the air around them vibrating with the insistent thump of bass and the chiding of an angry rapper to quit putting up with this shit and go ice a cop. They passed around a joint and drank beer from quart bottles and watched me with hooded eyes.

I parked the Olds at the curb and crossed the packed dirt yard to the Chevy. Four brown faces, suspicious and alert. Their hands were low, out of sight. Rap music pounded my ears and resonated inside my chest.

I took out a twenty, creased it lengthwise down the middle, and laid it on the window ledge near the driver's face. He was the oldest of the four, maybe seventeen. He had a wispy mustache that would someday look like Pancho Villa's, if he lived long enough. He glanced from me to the twenty, then reached over and shut off the noise.

"What's this?"

"For turning down the music," I said.

He took it.

I got out another twenty and said, "This is for telling me who lives in the end unit."

"You a fuckin' cop?"

"Do I look like a cop?"

"Yeah, motherfucker, you do."

"I can't help it, I was born this way. Who lives there?"

The twenty disappeared. "Anglo motherfucker named Granger."

"Is he a friend of yours?"

"He don't bother us, and we don't bother him."

"Is he home now?"

"Go ask him." He reached over and turned up the volume loud enough to jangle my eyes in their sockets.

I let the pounding bass push me toward Jack's unit. I mounted the creaking porch, and slid the Smith & Wesson Chief's Special from my hip holster, shielding my movement from the kids in the Chevy. Not that I thought they'd call the cops, no matter what they saw, but why take a chance?

I pulled open the drooping screen and knocked on the door. The snub-nosed revolver felt like a toy in my hand—it weighs less than twenty ounces and carries only five rounds. Of course, they're .38 Special cartridges, so you only need one. But really, I wasn't planning on using *any*, just poking the barrel in Jack's eye and asking him some pointed questions.

I knocked again.

No answer.

I put my ear to the door. Silence. Except for the booming rap music from the Chevy. And a baby squalling from inside the unit next to Jack's. And the rush of traffic on Federal Boulevard, honest citizens heading home from work.

I closed the screen, put away the gun, and stepped off the porch. It groaned.

I walked around the side of Jack's unit, trying to peek through the shaded windows. When I got to the rear, a little brown dog started yapping at me. His chain was wrapped around a clothesline pole in the sun behind the middle unit, and he made enough noise to bring out the neighbors. Nobody seemed to care. At one of Jack's rear windows I could see through a part in the ragged curtains—a dim kitchen, smaller even than mine. I checked the door lock. It looked easy enough.

I considered going in right then and waiting for him to come home. But there were a few items I wanted to pick up first from a hardware store.

Besides, this was Tuesday. Chess night.

Before I left, I got the dog unwrapped from his pole. He wasn't much more than a puppy. He wagged his tail and jumped all over me while I dumped the scummy water from his bowl, filled it at the outside tap, and set it next to the house in the shade.

"There you go, boy."

He peed on my shoe. No good deed goes unpunished.

On the way home I made one stop at a hardware store. Then I dropped by Vaz's apartment. Sophia answered the door. She's a short, robust, busty lady in her sixties with iron-gray hair and soft brown eyes.

"Jacob, come in."

"Hi, Sophia. Is Vaz around?"

"Yes, yes, I have him in the kitchen, slicing cucumbers for a salad. It's too hot to cook. Will you stay and eat?"

"Well, I . . ."

She grabbed my hand and dragged me into the apartment. "Vassily, Jacob is here! He'll be joining us for dinner!"

"I should wash up first."

"Use our bathroom. You know where it is."

With the door closed, I removed my jacket, unclipped the holster, and jammed it and the piece in an outside pocket. Sophia hates guns.

During our dinner (a heaping salad of garden vegetables and crabmeat, hard-crusted bread, and chilled white wine) Sophia asked me if I'd met the new tenant. Asked me knowingly. She is troubled by my bachelor status.

"Yes. This morning."

"She's a lovely girl, Jacob."

"Sophia . . ." Vaz rolled his eyes and shook his head.

Sophia shushed him and smiled at me. "Did you ask her out?"

"Um, well, no."

"But you will."

"Gee, I don't know, Sophia. I'll see how it goes. She's quite a bit younger than I am."

"Oh, tush." She reached over and patted me on the arm. "You're a young man, Jacob."

"Not so young anym—"

"I know," she said brightly. "The four of us could have dinner together. I'll bake a nice salmon. How does that sound?"

"Well . . ."

"Sometime soon, Jacob?"

Sigh. "Sure, why not."

"Good." Then she gave Vaz a look that said, *You see?*

I changed the subject and asked Vaz about the Denver chess club.

"Yes, they still meet on Tuesday nights," he said. "But since they've moved out to west Denver, I don't go as often as I used to. I don't like driving too far at night."

Which is the chess club's loss, because Vaz is a semiretired grandmaster. Formerly of the Soviet Union, he was ranked right up there with Petrossian and Spassky. Years ago, he and Sophia defected to the West during a tournament in Iceland, and they eventually settled at the foot of the Rockies, which Vaz said reminded him somewhat of the hills of home. I play him occasionally. Once I even managed to hold him to a draw. Of course, his back was to the board and his Queen was still in the box.

"How'd you like to go there with me tonight?"

His eyebrows rose like kittens arching their backs. "Are you getting serious about chess?"

"Just about one particular player."

15

By the time Vaz and I headed toward west Denver the sun had dropped below the jagged line of mountains. The air was already noticeably cooler. At this altitude it doesn't hold the heat for long.

I'd already told Vaz about Blyleven, but when I showed him his photograph—surprise, surprise—Vaz remembered him.

Actually, I shouldn't have been surprised. To reach the higher levels of chess, you need more than a deep understanding of the game, extreme self-confidence, and a killer instinct. You also need a terrific memory. Not just to memorize openings and multiple variations and critical positions—but entire games. And not only the hundreds, perhaps thousands of games that you've played, but thousands more than you've read about. Vaz once told me that he could replay from memory, move for move, every game he'd ever played, plus tell me the name of his opponent, the name of the tournament (if any), and the tournament champion (if not himself).

"Dates, though, I'm not too good with. I could only guess."

"Hey, nobody's perfect."

Vaz remembered seeing Blyleven at the club. He had never played him, though. Chess players tend to compete with opponents of similar levels—certainly in tournaments, and generally in pick-up games at clubs. Vaz playing Blyleven would have been like Nolan Ryan throwing heaters to a Little Leaguer. Not much fun for either of them. In fact, the only reason he ever played *me* was because I was the only other person in our building who knew the game. And, of course, we were friends.

"Did you ever talk to him?"

"I might have said hello," Vaz said.

"Do you remember anything about him?"

"I'm sorry, Jacob, no. Just his face. I know I've seen him at the club before. But not where we're going. They used to meet at a community center on East Thirteenth Avenue. That's where I saw him. But maybe someone tonight can help you."

"That's what I'm counting on."

"You shouldn't expect too much, though, Jacob. People come and go."

The club met in a run-down VFW building in northwest Denver. The large room in back had uneven lighting, a scuffed tile floor, and enough battered tables and chairs to seat a hundred. We were early, so there were only half a dozen other people.

They all knew Vaz, of course.

He introduced me to Ed Koepke, the club president, a sad-faced guy in his forties with a high forehead, a soft-looking paunch, and a pallid complexion. He remembered Blyleven, too, but like Vaz, only the name and face.

"When some of the lower rated players show up," Koepke told me, "you can ask them."

An hour later the room was half filled. Except for one woman— a homely young lady wearing blue jeans and a Bronco's jersey (number 7, what else?)—all the chess players were men. They ranged in age from teens to sixties.

Most of them looked like what you would call "regular guys." That is, they probably had wives or girlfriends or boyfriends, and they liked to spend at least a little time outdoors—playing ball or walking the dog or sitting in the yard drinking a beer, maybe reading King or Chrichton or what's his name, Grisham. In other words, they had lives outside of chess.

The others, though, were different. They reminded me of those shy, furtive, pale-faced characters you see on the nightly news being led in chains by sheriff's deputies after they've shot up their last place of employment with an Uzi. *He seemed like such a nice young man,* his neighbors would say. *Kind of quiet, though. Kept to himself.*

It was one of these guys who finally remembered Martin Blyleven.

I sat across a chessboard from him in the corner of the room. The black and white plastic pieces were in disarray, the aftermath of a mighty battle in which Dorsey had been beaten by the woman in orange. That was his name. Dorsey.

"Yeah, I remember Martin Blyleven," he said. He sat on one hand, while the other hopped and twitched around the board like a long-legged, pale spider, snatching up chessmen and setting them firmly on their home squares. "I haven't seen him for a long time, though."

"He died," I said.

"Oh."

Everyone else in the room was either playing chess or kibitzing a game. Some of the games looked quite serious, with both players hunched forward, taking their time, moving carefully, then noting the move on a score sheet and punching the chess clock, which stopped their own time and started their opponent's. At a few boards there were speed matches, where the players banged their pieces to the board, then quickly slapped the clock. One of these games was going on at the next table. Vaz sat beside me and watched it.

Bang, slap. Bang, slap.

"Did you ever see Blyleven outside of the chess club?" I asked Dorsey.

"No. Only here. Or maybe it was at the community center where we used to play. I was in a couple of tournaments with him, that's why I remember his face. And his name, when you said it. Blyleven."

"Did he have any close friends?"

Bang, slap. Bang, slap.

"I couldn't say," Dorsey said.

Terrific. Although I don't really know what I'd expected to find here. "Was there anyone who he seemed to hang out with more than others, studying games, or whatever?"

"I don't remember."

I started to get up. "Well, thanks for—"

"You know, there was one guy."

Bang, slap.

"Oh?"

"I don't remember his name. But he had this skin thing on his face, kind of weird looking. I played him once. Maybe in the same tournament with Blyleven."

"Which tournament," Vaz said, startling both Dorsey and me.

Dorsey thought for a minute, then said, "The Holiday Open." He couldn't suppress a thin smile. "I tied for second place."

"In which section?" Vaz wanted to know.

"The 'under sixteen-hundred.' "

"I'll be a moment, Jacob."

Vaz left us and wound his way between tables to Koepke, who was watching a game in progress. Vaz drew him aside. I saw Koepke nod his head, then lead Vaz to a dais at the far end of the room. A table was set up there with a laptop computer and a printer. Koepke's portable office.

I asked Dorsey, "What sort of skin thing?"

"What?"

"On this man's face."

"Oh. Like a bad burn, pink and purple and puckered up, all over his neck and chin."

"Besides that, what did he look like? Black, white? Big, small? Young, old?

"He was white, about average size, I guess. Older. About your age."

Oh, thanks. "And he and Blyleven were friends?"

"I think so. I saw them together a few times at the club."

"Did they arrive together?"

"I don't know." He stared past me and waved at someone. "Look, I'm supposed to play this guy tonight."

"Okay, just tell me, is there anything else you remember about this man and Blyleven?"

He scrunched up his face and thought. "All I remember is after the Holiday Open we were talking about the tournament and replaying some of the games, and—"

"You and who?"

"Blyleven and the man with the burns. I'd played against them both, and we were analyzing our games. I got the impression that Blyleven and this other man didn't know each other too well then, but after that they seemed to get real friendly. In fact, a few weeks later—and this is the only thing I can remember, okay?, and then I have to start my game—a few weeks later I saw them sitting together, talking, laughing, and I went over to see what was up. But it had nothing to do with chess."

"What was it?"

"Germany."

"Germany? The country?"

"Yeah."

"What about it?"

"I don't know. All I remember is they were talking about Germany. Look, I'm really supposed to play this guy."

He nodded toward a skinny character with inch-thick eyeglasses standing behind me. I was in his seat. I stood and told Dorsey, "Thanks for your help."

Vaz was alone on the dais, looking through several pages of computer print-outs.

I went up there and asked him, "What's that?"

"The tournament record and some of the score sheets from the Holiday Open four years ago. Actually, four and a half—the tournament was in January."

"Koepke has four years worth of records stored on that little computer?"

Vaz gave me an annoyed look. "Jacob, that's a four-hundred meg hard drive."

"Yeah, whatever."

"The tournament was a Swiss-type," Vaz said, "and each player had four matches. Dorsey tied for second place, as he said. He played Martin Blyleven and three others. Here, I wrote down their names."

He handed me a scrap of paper with scribbles on it.

"I can't read this."

"Never mind, I can. Also, I had Ed print out all four of Blyleven's games." He showed me pages filled with columns of letters and numbers—the moves of each game.

"Why?"

He shrugged. "Perhaps they will tell us something about the man."

I didn't see how. But this was Vaz's territory, not mine.

"Let's ask Dorsey about these names."

Dorsey and his pal had not yet started their game, but they were itching to do so. Vaz read off the names of Dorsey's four opponents in the Holiday Open.

"What was the third one again?"

"Stan Lessing," Vaz said.

Dorsey nodded. "That's him, the guy with the burns. And there's something else I remembered."

"What?"

"That time I heard them talking about Germany, remember?"

"A few weeks after the Holiday Open," I said.

"Right, well, after that I didn't see either one of them again. They stopped coming to the club."

"You're sure?"

"Positive."

Vaz and I sat at a vacant table, and Vaz set up a chessboard. He played through all four of Blyleven's games, talking to me in a low voice. Or maybe he was talking to himself, because his eyes moved only between the board and the score sheets.

"... e-four, c-five, knight f-three, knight c-six, d-four, pawn takes pawn, knight takes pawn, yes, yes, all book stuff, then here and here and here, black castles ..." Shuffling the pieces about the board. "... then rook comes over, pawn moves, oh, but this is weak, bishop here, and queen takes ..." And so it went for the better part of an hour.

When he was finished, he heaved a sigh and sat back from the board, looking like a college professor who had just finished grading term papers, and poor ones at that.

"Well?"

"It's not very good chess, Jacob. I daresay you could do well against any of these players."

"Gee, thanks. Is that it?"

"Well, I can tell you this about Blyleven. He plays two vastly different styles, depending on whether he's white or black."

"Isn't that the nature of the game?"

"Yes, of course. White moves first and so has the initiative. Black must defend, and at some point he must counter white's attack or be crushed. But Blyleven takes it to an extreme."

"What do you mean?"

"In this tournament he played two games as black, and two as white. When he was black, he was overly cautious, timid, you might say, making small, careful moves, hardly even venturing onto his opponent's side of the board. But as white, he went completely the other way, extremely aggressive, throwing caution to the wind, totally committing himself to the attack, no matter how unsound."

"Which method paid off?"

"He had two draws with black. With white he won one and lost one. But I'll tell you something, Jacob, it is almost like two different players here. One is meek and careful, the other violently aggressive."

So much for Blyleven the chess player. I wondered which description best fit Blyleven the man.

Vaz bid good night to his friends, and we drove home.

Along the way he asked me, "Do you think Stan Lessing has anything to do with your case?"

"I'd say the odds are good. As soon as he and Blyleven became friends, they stopped going to the chess club. And two months later Blyleven's plane blew up. Also, Vivian was certain that Blyleven played chess *every* Tuesday until the plane crash. Obviously, he was lying to her. And if he wasn't playing chess, where was he?"

"With Stan Lessing."

"That's my guess."

"What do you make of Blyleven and Lessing talking about Germany?"

"I have no idea, Vaz. But there's something else. Probably only a coincidence."

"What?"

"Lessing's face had been severely burned, and Blyleven's body—or whoever's body it was—was burned beyond recognition."

Vaz shook his head. "That's a stretch, Jacob."

"I guess."

When I got to the apartment building, I double-parked in front. "Aren't you coming in?"

"I have one more stop to make," I said. "Thanks for coming with me tonight."

"I enjoyed it. Good night, Jacob."

"Good night."

I waited until he had gone up the poorly lighted walk, unlocked the front door, and stepped inside.

Then I headed to north Denver to see my good friend Jack.

16

It was a little before ten when I turned east off Federal Boulevard. I drove past Jack's triplex, continued on to the end of the block, and parked the Olds around the corner. The streetlamp was dead, but the neighborhood was fairly well lighted by city glow. I unlocked the trunk and shoved a few handy tools of the trade in my jacket pockets. Then I lifted out a hefty paper bag. It was filled with goodies I'd purchased that afternoon at the hardware store.

Never visit a friend's house empty-handed.

I walked back toward Jack's place. It was a pleasant, still night. Pale light from TV sets flickered in front windows along the way. Most people in the neighborhood had settled in to watch the evening news and maybe Letterman before heading to bed.

The end units of the triplex were dark—so Jack wasn't home, and the gang-bangers I'd seen earlier were probably out cruising the streets. The window shades in the middle unit glowed with yellow light. I hoped they'd brought their puppy in for the night.

They had.

The backyard was empty and quiet. Diffused light from the neighbors' windows fell on the clothesline pole, the limp chain, the water bowl . . . and Jack's back door. It took me longer to get the pick out of my pocket than it did to open the lock. I stepped into the kitchen and closed the door behind me.

Enough light came through the flimsy curtains for me to make out shapes: refrigerator, sink, table, two chairs, doorway.

I put the sack on the table and clicked on my small flashlight. Then I moved from the kitchen, keeping the yellow-white circle of light at my feet.

The doorway led into a minuscule hallway. There was another doorway straight ahead into the living room, and open doors to the right (bathroom) and left (bedroom).

I checked the bedroom first. The double bed was unmade, with the sheets tossed back from one side and one of the two pillows on the floor. In the closet I found a winter coat, a lightweight zippered jacket, a pair of pants hung crookedly on a hanger, and three shirts. Jack was not a clothes horse. The secondhand dressing table held nothing but smelly socks and underwear, a couple of sweaters and T-shirts, and a switchblade knife with a six-inch blade.

I slipped the knife into my pocket.

Then I poked my head in the bathroom. There was a dank, fetid odor. A scummy shower curtain hung limply around a filthy bathtub. The toilet seat was up, but hey, so was mine. The door to the medicine cabinet hung open. Inside were a couple of throwaway safety razors, a sticky-looking comb, and a half-full bottle of aspirin. On top of the sink lay a toothbrush and a deformed tube of toothpaste. I guess even scumbags clean their teeth.

The living room was furnished in Neo-Goodwill—a sagging couch, a battered chair, and a coffee table littered with empty beer cans. On top of the TV set in the corner was a small plastic box. At least he had cable.

I sat in the chair in the semidarkness and waited for him to come home.

The neighbors' TV entertained me with a muted mumble. An hour later all was quiet.

At 11:30 a siren screamed by on Federal Boulevard.

At 12:20 a car passed in front of the triplex.

At 2:15 a car stopped out front.

I stood and moved beside the door. I didn't dare risk a peek through the front window shade because he might see the movement. A car door creaked open, then chunked closed. I waited, putting my weight on the balls of my feet, flexing my shoulders and fingers, getting ready.

Suddenly, there came a loud sound from the kitchen. Shit. It hadn't occurred to me that Jack would walk around to the back door. I hustled into the kitchen. And discovered my stupid mistake. The sound I'd heard was the refrigerator kicking on. Now it chugged merrily away.

The front door opened. The living-room light came on.

I stood beside the kitchen doorway and slipped the sap from my jacket pocket. It's a leather-wrapped, ten-ounce lead disk at the end of a spring-loaded grip. Payback's a bitch, ain't it?

I heard Jack go into the bathroom and piss and fart at the same time. The toilet flushed. I wondered if he'd go straight to bed or watch TV for a while or come into the kitchen for a nightcap.

He stepped through the doorway, reaching for the light.

I nailed him, and down he went.

When I flipped the switch, the room filled with a sickly yellow glow. Quickly, I opened the sack on the table and got out the roll of duct tape—another nice irony, I thought. I flopped him over on his stomach. He moaned, and gave me a whiff of whiskey. I pulled his arms behind him and taped his wrists together, running the tape in a cross pattern, between and around. Then I hoisted him off the floor. He was short, but compact and heavy, and I had to strain to get him into one of the kitchen chairs.

"Huh?" He blinked, trying to focus his eyes.

I pulled his arms up and over the chair, so that the back stuck up between his elbows. Then I started wrapping tape around his chest and arms and the back of the chair to keep him in place.

"What the fuck?" He shook his head. "Hey!"

"No talking," I said, and slapped a strip of tape over his mouth.

He struggled with his bonds and cursed me behind his gag. Then he leaned forward and stood, hunched over, with the chair still taped to his back, as if he thought he could run away. I took out the sap and showed it to him.

"Please sit."

He glared at me. Then he sat.

I squatted before him and started to tape his ankle to the chair leg. He tried to kick me.

"Hey, Jack, I'm going to do this either while you're awake or while you're out cold. What's it going to be?"

I gave him a few seconds to think it over, then I taped his ankles to the chair legs.

"Now we can talk." I pulled the tape from his mouth, letting it hang from his cheek by one end.

"Fuck you," he said.

"Why are you looking for Martin Blyleven?"

"Fuck you."

"Where can I find Manny?"

"Fuck you."

"Jack, Jack, Jack. I hope that's the whiskey talking."

I slapped the tape over his mouth, dragged him and the chair to the wall, and tipped him back so that the front legs and his feet were off the floor. I untied one of his grubby athletic shoes and pulled it off.

"Whew. Time for Odor-Eaters, don't you think?"

I tried to peel off his sock, but I'd taped it to his leg. I took out the switchblade and clicked it open. Jack's eyes grew wide.

"Don't worry," I said. "I'm not going to stick you. It's not my style."

I carefully cut off his soiled sock, revealing a stubby foot, as pale and blue-veined as a cave fish. I folded the knife and put it away. Then I opened the paper sack on the table and withdrew a small propane tank.

"Here we are."

It was a shiny blue steel cylinder, about eighteen inches long and three inches in diameter. The nozzle poked straight out the top end for a few inches, then bent at a forty-five-degree angle. I turned the brass knob at the base of the nozzle. Gas hissed. It sounded evil, even to me. I struck a match, held it near the nozzle, and the gas ignited in a long, pale-blue flame. I adjusted the knob, slowly bringing the flame in until the tip was as hard and pointed as a blue spike.

"Perfect."

I squatted before Jack's bare foot. He watched me with wild eyes, breathing rapidly through his nose.

"Actually, I didn't have to take off your shoe, you know."

I picked it up and held the point of the flame to the sole. The synthetic rubber began to smoke and crackle and drip. It took less than a minute to burn a hole completely through. A rancid, eye-watering odor hung in the air.

"Believe me, it would stink a lot more if your foot was still inside."

I tossed the smoldering shoe in the sink. Then I carefully set the tank and its hungry flame on the floor where Jack could see it. He watched me with great interest, all traces of whiskey fog burned away.

I was fairly sure he was ready to talk. But I wanted to be absolutely certain. Because there was no way in hell I wanted to go through with this. Not with Jack, not with anybody.

I said, "The guy at the hardware store told me the tank held enough for two hours or so. But you seem like a tough guy, and I didn't know if that would be enough." I lifted another tank from the sack. "So I bought two. One for each foot."

I dragged the other chair before him and sat down.

"Here's what we'll do. I'll ask a question, and you answer. If I don't like the answer I'll burn a hole in your foot and ask it again. How does that sound?"

His eyes moved from my face to the propane tank and back. They stayed there.

"Oh, right, the tape." I peeled it gently from his mouth, and the words spilled out.

"None of it was my idea, I was just hired to do a job, I've got nothing against you personally, I was just following orders, okay? Manny paid me and Wedge and we did what—"

"Slow down. Why are you looking for Martin Blyleven?"

"*I'm* not looking for him. I don't even know who the fuck he is. It's Manny's show."

"What's Manny's full name?"

"I don't know."

"Oh, Jack." I reached down for the propane tank.

"Listen to me, goddammit! I never saw the guy in my life before yesterday. He's up here from Tucson."

"Oh?"

"That's all I know about him. Other than he's connected."

"Connected? You mean Mafia?"

Jack nodded. "They tell me he's a stone-cold killer, although you wouldn't know it to look at him."

"Who's *they?*"

"Fat Pauli DaNucci. His people, I mean."

"That's who hired you?"

Jack nodded. "Me and Wedge sometimes get business from him. Well, not him directly, but through his people. Collecting gambling debts and so on. Nothing big. You can't get into the big stuff unless you're a pie-zon."

"Why does DaNucci want Blyleven?"

"*He* doesn't want him. It's someone in Arizona, the one who sent Manny. The way I get it is DaNucci is just doing a favor for this big-deal Mafia guy down there, letting him hire some of his part-time muscle. Me and Wedge."

I knew who DaNucci was, most people around Denver did. A big frog in a little pond. Denver was more or less in the center of a vast wasteland, as far as the Mafia was concerned, with Las Vegas to the west, Kansas City to the east, Minneapolis to the north, and Phoenix (or maybe now it was Tucson) to the south. DaNucci had no real power outside of this small province. But if any of the big guys did business here, they talked to him first. He might be small, but his guns could kill you just as dead as theirs.

"Who's the guy in Arizona?"

"I don't know his name."

"But you're sure he's the one who sent Manny."

He nodded, glancing at the blue flame waiting patiently near his foot. "After we left your apartment yesterday, he mentioned it. 'My boss in Tucson isn't going to like this' is what he said."

"Why does Manny want Blyleven?"

"I told you, I don't know."

"And you've never heard of Martin Blyleven before?"

"Never."

"What about Lawrence Foster?" The pilot.

"No."

"Or Stan Lessing?" The chess player.

"Him neither."

"When you were in my apartment, Manny said I'd been asking questions around town about Blyleven. Who told him that?"

"I don't know. Well, wait." Jack frowned. "He did say something."

"What?"

"When we went to your place, I asked him who you were. He said he'd never heard of you before. So I asked him how he was sure you were the guy he wanted. He gave me this funny sort of smile, cold, you know? And he said, 'Would God lie?' "

"What's that supposed to mean?"

"How the fuck should I know? But those were his exact words."

"Where is Manny now?"

"I don't know."

"Did he go back to Tucson?"

"You wish." Jack actually smirked—a difficult thing to do when you're wrapped in duct tape, tipped back in a chair, and wearing only one shoe. "He's not through with you yet."

"Meaning what?"

"He paid off me and Wedge, three hundred apiece. Said he didn't need us anymore. Said he could deal with you himself."

"Deal with me."

"That's what he said."

Swell. "But you and Wedge are out of it."

"We are now."

I clicked open the switchblade. "Because if I thought you weren't . . ."

"Hey, look," he said quickly, his smirk a distant memory, "as far as I'm concerned, you and I are square, okay? I hit you and you hit me. You'll never see me again."

I guess I believed him. Not that there was much I could do about it now. I sure as hell couldn't turn him into the cops, not after what I'd done here. So I turned off the propane tank, set his chair down on all fours, and cut the tape from his ankles and chest.

He stood and turned sideways, holding out his taped wrists.

I packed up my toys in the paper sack. I left Jack's knife on the table.

"Hey. My hands."

"If you can't cut yourself loose, Jack, go next door and ask for help. But wait until a decent hour, all right? People are sleeping over there."

I left him standing in the kitchen, his shoe still smoldering in the sink.

17

On Wednesday morning I woke up tired. Four hours sleep isn't what it used to be.

But after half a hundred push-ups, twice as many sit-ups, a quick shower, and a shave I felt okay. I wondered how Jack felt. A lump on his head and a hole in his shoe. It sounded like a country-and-western song. I was a little troubled, though, by what I might have done if he'd refused to talk. How far would I have gone with the propane burner? I wasn't really sure. But he *did* talk, so forget about it.

What mattered was what he'd told me.

The Mafia was looking for Blyleven.

And not just looking, I'd wager. They'd sent Manny to kill him. In fact, it was even possible they'd blown up the plane four years ago to get him. They'd assumed he was dead, until I started poking around and asking questions. Now they wanted to settle unfinished business.

The question was, why?

As far as I knew there were only two reasons the Mafia kills people. Money or revenge.

So what was the connection between Blyleven, a mild-mannered church accountant, and the Mafia? Had he been moonlighting as a drug dealer? Or a bookie? It seemed unlikely. But then, you never knew.

There was one definite connection, though.

Tucson.

The mob boss in Tucson had sent Manny to get Blyleven. Blyleven's employer, the Church of the Nazarene, ran a relief organization known as World Flock out of Tucson. In fact, Blyleven had been on his way to Tucson when he died—or at least, when his plane had blown up.

There was another connection, if you could call it that. When Jack had asked Manny how he knew I was the guy he wanted, Manny said, "Would God lie?" And Blyleven's last employer was a man of God.

Vaz would call that a stretch.

I knew a few people who were familiar with things in Arizona. Their numbers were at my office.

Before I left, though, I hunted up George the caretaker to give him a gift. Three gifts, actually—a nearly new roll of duct tape and two propane tanks, one slightly used. I found him in the backyard.

The yard is longer than it is wide, bordered by immense lilac bushes that have all but engulfed an old iron fence. A pair of majestic oaks shade most of the lawn. The sunniest area is in the rear, next to the alley. Mrs. Finch's vegetable garden. The morning was bright and clear, and there was a fresh smell in the air. That would soon change, however. George was pouring gasoline in the tank of his ancient lawn mower.

"How's it going, George?"

"It ain't goin' at all. Not until I fill her with gas."

A comedian. "Here. I brought you something."

He straightened up—well, as straight as his old bones would allow—and eyed the bag suspiciously. He wore overalls, a white T-shirt, a long-billed cap with a faded Mack truck logo, and thick-soled work boots. The skin on his face and arms was loose and brown and more wrinkled than the paper sack I held out to him.

"What've you got there?"

I opened the sack and showed him. "Can you use these?"

"I suppose I could." But he made no move to take the sack. George always figures there are strings attached.

"Good. Take them, they're yours."

He squinted one eye. "Why are you giving them to me?"

"Because you can use them and I can't."

"What are you doing with these things, anyway?"

"I, ah, needed them for a job."

"You didn't do nothing up in your apartment, did you?"

"No, George, I—"

"Because *I'm* the one who takes care of things around here, and Mrs. Finch don't want nobody else messing with the plumbing and such."

"Got it." I pushed the sack at him.

He took it reluctantly. "Just what sort of job were you doing with this, anyway?"

"Does it matter?"

"It might."

"Okay, I had to tape a guy up and threaten to burn his foot."

He gaped at me. And then he burst out laughing, showing me his dentures. "That's a good one."

"See you later, George."

I left him grinning from ear to ear, yanking on the mower's pull-start. ". . . tape a guy and burn his foot. Hah!"

When I walked around to the front of the house, the mailman was just handing Mrs. Finch a stack of envelopes. We tenants don't have our own mailboxes. This is Mrs. Finch's house and, by God, she's going to take in the mail. She likes to separate it and lay it out in neat little piles on a table in the foyer, as a service to us. Also, this allows her to see who's getting what from whom. I had one piece—a Manila envelope with the FBI logo printed in the corner.

Mrs. Finch handed it to me. But when I tried to take it, she didn't let go.

"I hope you remember what I told you yesterday," she hissed, looking pointedly past me.

Sharon Hoffman was just emerging from her apartment. Today she wore skintight jeans and a loose tank top that was scooped low enough to show off the tops of her breasts. There was plenty to show.

Too young, Lomax, much too young, no matter what Sophia says.

Sharon said, "Good morning." She gave us each a friendly smile.

Especially me. No, really.

"Hi," I said.

Mrs. Finch went, "Humph."

Sharon glanced at the mail on the table. "Anything for me?" She looked at me when she said it. A *knowing* look, too. I swear.

"Nothing," Mrs. Finch said.

"I'm having a few people over tonight," Sharon said to me. "Sort of a housewarming. I'd love it if you'd come."

"Well, maybe I—"

"A *party*?" Mrs. Finch glared up at her. "I don't like my tenants making a racket with loud music and such."

"Oh, we'll be very quiet," Sharon said. Then to me, "Come any time after eight. Or before, for that matter." Again the knowing look, I'm not kidding.

"I'll try to make it."

She looked down at Mrs. Finch. "Of course, you're invited, too."

"Humph." Mrs. Finch stomped into her apartment and slammed the door.

Sharon smiled at me. "See you tonight, then?" She shot one hip. What a hip!

"I'll try." I walked out with my ears buzzing. Get a grip, for chrissake.

At the office the red light on my answering machine was blinking. I tossed the unopened Manila envelope on the desk and hit the playback button.

"Hello, it's Nora Foster. I finally remembered what Larry told me about Martin Blyleven's briefcase. Call me at noon, or this evening, if you like. I'll be home for lunch, and then I work until five. Good-bye. Oh, it's Wednesday morning, about seven-thirty. Good-bye."

It was nearly nine now, but I tried her number anyway. No answer.

She'd said that her husband mentioned something peculiar about Blyleven's leather briefcase. I couldn't imagine what it was. A case was a case. Why didn't she just describe it in her phone message? Too complicated? No matter, because there were a few other things I wanted to discuss with her.

I slit open the Manila envelope.

There was no note, nothing with Agent Cochran's name on it, nothing to tie him to me. All he'd sent was a photocopy of ten fingerprints and two palm prints. At the bottom of the slick sheet was Martin E. Blyleven's name, date of birth, enlistment date in the U.S. Army, and serial number.

The prints were useless to me. Sure, I'd had some brief training in fingerprint technique when I'd been a Denver cop—mostly lectures on where fingerprints might be found at a crime scene and how to preserve that area until the experts showed up. But even assuming I had a latent print from the blackmailer, it would take a specialist to make a positive comparison between the arches, loops, and whorls in these inked prints and any latent ones. Although . . .

I found a magnifying glass in one of my desk drawers and took a closer look at the prints.

In the center of the finger pads there were very definite whorls made up of four of five concentric circles. I looked at my own finger pad. Arches, not whorls.

Let's say I *could* get the blackmailer to leave his fingerprints— don't ask me how, maybe get him to send something to Vivian. Then I could dust the prints with powder and lift them with Scotch tape. Hell, even *I* could tell whether or not they had whorls similar to these. If they didn't, then the blackmailer wasn't Blyleven, pure and simple. Of course, if he did have whorls, it still didn't mean he was Blyleven. It only meant I'd had to bring in an expert. In other words, the cops. And that was something that Vivian and Roger Armis did not want to do. Neither did I. At least, not at this point.

So forget about the prints.

But all was not lost. There was Blyleven's service number. Maybe I could find out what he'd done in the Army. Like fly a plane. Or handle explosives.

I pawed through my meager bookcase looking for a particular directory.

I'm a dues-paying member of the World Association of Detectives, the Society of Professional Investigators, and the Association of Licensed Detectives (although in this state you don't need a license to practice—which will give you some idea of what Colorado thinks of PIs). Each of these associations publishes a list of members. I've called some of them for help in the past. And some of them have even called me, so there you are.

One agency that came to mind was Lifkin Investigations in Washington, D.C. A few years ago Mr. Lifkin himself had given me a call to help find a child-support-owing husband thought to have recently moved to the Denver area. I did a quick check with the phone company and the post office, but the deadbeat was not going to make it that easy. He had to be living somewhere, though. And if it was a house or apartment, he had to have gas and electricity. One phone call to Public Service gave me the guy's address.

I hadn't even charged Lifkin for my services, figuring a future favor would be worth more than an hour's billing. I had no doubt that he'd remember me.

I found his number and dialed him up.

"Hi, Mr. Lifkin? This is Jake Lomax calling from Denver."

"Thank you for calling Lifkin Investigations, Mr. Lohmaus. How may I help you?"

"That's Lo*max*." So much for his memory.

I told him I wanted the service record for Martin Blyleven, birth date so-and-so, serial number such-and-such. He said he could probably have it by the end of the day.

"What is your billing address?" he asked me.

"You don't remember me, do you?"

"Should I?"

"I did a little work for you three or four years ago."

"That must have been my father. He's retired."

"Oh."

"What is your billing address?"

I gave him my office address and told him I'd call him back before six P.M. his time.

Then I flipped through the Rolodex for my man in Arizona.

Hal Zimmerman had worked for both Denver dailies before

moving south to escape the winter's snow and cold. Who could blame him? On the other hand, who'd want to spend their summers where it was hot enough to melt asphalt?

The switchboard put me through to him at the city desk.

"Hal. Jake Lomax."

"Hey, Jake, how you doing?"

Hal and I had first run into each other when I was just starting out in the PI business. At the time we were both looking for the same guy but for different reasons, and our paths had crossed several times. Finally, we threw in together, shared information, and made certain promises to each other: I wouldn't grant interviews with any other reporters, and he would leave my client's name out of his story. It had worked out well. My client was introduced to her long-lost father, and Hal won an award for his series "Adoption—Love Lost and Found."

We exchanged a few exaggerations, and then I asked him about the Mafia in Arizona.

"Joseph Scolla," he said without hesitation. "Or Joey the Jap as he's fondly known, due to the slight slant to his eyes. A reputed member of the Bonanno crime family. Don't you love that word? Reputed. He lives in Tucson, but he controls everything in the region."

"By everything, you mean . . . ?"

"Drugs, gambling, prostitution, loan sharking. You know, the four basic food groups."

"Does he have any interest up here?"

"In Colorado? Not that I've ever heard of. But who can say for sure. His type rarely talks to the media about business affiliations."

"Have you ever heard of Franklin Reed's Church of the Nazarene?"

He thought for a moment. "It sounds familiar."

"How about World Flock?"

"Sure. Oh yeah, that's right, World Flock is run by Reed. Headquartered in Tucson, right?"

"Right."

"Wait a minute. First you mention the Mafia and then World Flock. Are you suggesting there's a connection?"

"I'm not suggesting, I'm just wondering."

"Now that *would* be a story."

I told him about the plane crash four years ago, how Blyleven had been working for the church and World Flock, and that I'd been looking into his death.

"And out of nowhere comes this Mafia type," I said. "Well, not nowhere. Tucson. Blyleven had been on his way to Tucson when he died. Maybe there's a connection, maybe not."

"How do you know the man from Tucson is Mafia?"

"It's a long story, but trust me, I do. And he seems to have it in for me. He was sent by his 'boss,' who resides in Tucson and—"

"Who would be Joey the Jap."

"Presumably. And his name is Manny."

Hal hesitated. "Manny? Do you mean Anthony Mancusso?"

"I don't know."

"What does your Manny look like?"

I described him.

Hal exhaled audibly. "That sounds like Mancusso, all right. He works for Scolla. A very nasty character, this Manny. He's suspected in several gang-style murders down here. The victims were mutilated. I won't go into the gory details, but the medical examiner said it was done while they were still alive. Believe me, Jake, you don't want to mess with that guy."

"I'll try to keep that in mind. Meanwhile, you could do me a favor."

"Name it."

"See if you can find some tie, no matter how slight, between the Arizona mob and World Flock or Franklin Reed."

"I'll ask around and get back to you."

"I appreciate it, Hal."

"No problem. Hey, if anything comes out of this, we have the same deal as before, right?"

He meant he'd get an exclusive story and my clients wouldn't be mentioned.

"Same deal," I said, and rang off.

18

I guess I should've felt lucky to be alive.

But I doubted luck had anything to do with it. If Hal was right, Manny was a professional hit man, a stone-cold killer. He could have snuffed me in my apartment, no problem. And if that had been his intention, he wouldn't have been deterred by the intrusion of old Mrs. Finch.

So he wanted me alive. Probably hoping I'd lead him to Blyleven.

Which meant he was nearby, watching me.

Maybe I should lead him in a circle, get behind him, and deal with him the way I'd dealt with Jack. Then I could ask him all the tough questions. Why does the Mafia want Blyleven dead? Who blew up the plane four years ago? Did it involve World Flock and Franklin Reed?

There were a few problems with talking to Manny, though. First of all, it would be difficult if not impossible to ambush him. He was too crafty a predator to let himself be easily trapped. Second, even if I somehow managed to knock him down and tie him up, I doubted that he'd be as cooperative as Jack. He'd spit in my eye. And third, it was quite likely he didn't know all the answers. He didn't *need* to know them. He'd been hired to do a job. And when guys like Manny are told to kill somebody, they don't ask, ''Why do you want him dead?

What did he do to deserve it?'' No, they ask only one question: "Where is he?''

Manny was hoping I'd answer it for him.

But who could answer my questions?

I'd bet that Joseph Scolla could. Or course, even if I went to Tucson, it was doubtful that Joey the Jap would grant me an interview.

There was someone else, though, much closer to home.

I phoned the Church of the Nazarene and asked for Reverend Reed. I got as far as Matthew Styles.

"How may I help you, Mr. Lomax?''

"Grant me an audience with your boss.''

"I'm afraid Pastor Reed is tied up for the rest of the day.''

"Tell him it has to do with Joseph Scolla.''

He hesitated. "Who?''

He knew. "A friend of Reed's in Tucson. Go ask him. I'll hold.''

He hesitated again. "Just a moment.''

I listened to dead air for ten minutes before Styles came back on the line. "As it happens,'' he said with forced nonchalance, "Pastor Reed has a break in his schedule at three this afternoon.''

"I'll be there.''

"Not at the church. The reverend will meet you at his home.''

He gave me the address. Not exactly the poor side of town.

"Please don't be late,'' he said, and hung up.

So Reed and Styles knew Scolla. But why were they being so obvious about it? Styles could've simply hung up. Maybe Reed wanted to find out exactly how much I knew. The trouble was, I knew very little. I needed to pick up a few more facts before I met with him.

I dialed a number in Castle Rock. A young girl answered.

"May I speak to Earl?''

"Grandpa's working in the garden. Hang on and I'll go get him.''

"I'll call later,'' I said. In person.

There were large, cottony clouds floating over the hills west of Castle Rock. Nothing like the thunderheads I'd seen on my visit a few days ago. I parked before the two-story brick house, went up to the porch, and rang the bell.

The screen was latched, but the front door was open. The house looked quiet and empty. An invitation to a burglary. If it had been Denver. But this was a small town, and people still trusted each other.

I rang again and waited.

No answer.

I walked around the side of the house.

A thigh-high white picket fence enclosed the backyard. It was half lawn and half garden. There were rows of corn stalks as tall as a man, a trellis thick with pea vines, tomato plants pushing through their chicken-wire cages, heads of lettuce, onions, pump-kins, acorn squash, carrots, and a few other rows of leafy plants—maybe turnips or beets. The growing season here runs from about Memorial Day to a little after Labor Day, and Earl Wilson was making the most of it.

At the moment, he was on his hands and knees, hunting weeds.

I unlatched the little gate and crossed the yard, calling "Good morning" as I went.

Earl gave a start when he saw me. Then he went back to his weeding.

He was wearing brown denim pants that had been washed a hundred times and a faded blue work shirt with ragged, cut-off sleeves. There were dark blue sweat stains down the middle of his back and under his arms, and the nape of his neck was the color of terra cotta, a burn over a tan. He also wore a battered ball cap and gloves soiled with clean earth. He dug out a ground-hugging weed with a trowel and tossed it in a half-filled bucket.

"Nice garden." I stood between a pair of plants bursting with tomatoes.

He snorted, not looking at me. "What do you want here?"

So much for small talk. "There's something I need to clear up."

"What?"

"The night before the plane crash."

"I already told you all about that."

"I don't think you did."

He moved forward a few feet on his hands and knees and dug

out another weed. Then he sat back on his heels, still not looking at me. When he spoke, it sounded like a plea.

"Why don't you just leave me alone."

"Can't do it, Earl."

Slowly, he got to his feet. He dropped the trowel on the ground, then pulled off his gloves and dropped them, too. There were dark stains on his knees.

"I've got a nice family here," he said, looking me in the eye. "A wonderful daughter, a good son-in-law, and three beautiful grandkids. They don't give a damn about my past, do you understand? They love me for who I am. And they don't deserve to be hassled by you."

"Fine. Talk to me and I'll leave."

"Like I said, I've already told you everything."

"Not according to Vivian Armis."

"Who?"

"Martin Blyleven's widow."

He licked his lips and shifted his gaze. The bill of his cap dropped a shadow over his face, and his eyes seemed to be hiding in there. "What about her?"

"She told me that her husband went on a mysterious errand the night before the crash. It was late at night, and he was gone for several hours. I think he went to Centennial Airport to put a bomb on his plane."

He swallowed hard and said, "I wouldn't know anything about that."

"You're a liar."

His face darkened behind the shadow of his cap, and his hands bunched up into fists. "Don't you ever call me that." His voice was low and harsh. I thought he might take a swing at me.

"Go ahead, Earl, give it your best shot. You might even knock me down. But I'm not going away. Not until I have the truth."

He glared at me a moment longer, then he looked away. His shoulders seemed to sag.

I said, "Vivian Armis has kept that a secret for four years. She's told no one but her present husband and me. Not even the federal authorities. But if *I* told them ... well, you talk about being *hassled*. They'll swarm around you like flies."

He hesitated, pain in his face.

"Talk to me, Earl. It'll stay just between us, I promise."

"How can I be sure of that?" His voice was small.

"I guess you'll have to trust me."

He gazed out over his garden. When he spoke, it was almost as if I weren't there.

"I was a cop for twenty years," he said. "In all that time I never once took a bribe. And believe me, I was offered more than a few. Drug dealers, pimps, they were always loaded with cash, always ready to give you a share for looking the other way. But I never did, not once. I was a good cop. Okay, I drank. But I never cheated and I never stole. Same thing when I was a security guard. Always did my job, always played it straight." He paused. "Except for that one time."

"What happened, Earl?"

"Blyleven approached me one day," he said, still looking out over his rows of corn, as if he were addressing them not me. "I'd spoken to him before plenty of times, but not at length, you know? Just, 'Hi. How are you? Nice day.' Like that. But this time he pulls me aside, smiling and secretive, taking me into his confidence. He wants me to help him play a trick on Larry Foster. A surprise for Foster's birthday."

"His birthday."

"I know, I know," he said, half turning to face me. "It sounds stupid now. But at the time . . . Anyway, I knew Foster pretty well, knew he was a good guy, and besides . . ."

"What?"

He turned away again, not talking to me, hating to admit it to another person. "Blyleven offered me a thousand bucks. Said I could buy something nice for my grandkids."

"What did he want you to do?"

"Unlock the hangar at a certain time and stay away from it for an hour."

"And you did."

"Yes, yes, that one time I took the money. What was the harm? The aircraft belonged to Blyleven—well, to his church. I didn't think he was going to *steal* it. All he wanted to do was string some banners inside the plane, stuff like that, surprise Foster. At

first I said no, but he kept after me. He said Foster would get a
big kick out of it. 'Be a sport, Earl,' he kept saying. 'Be a sport.' ''

"When did he approach you?"

"A few days before the . . . explosion."

"Tell me about that night."

He heaved a sigh. "I did my normal rounds, and at eleven I
swung by the hangar and unlocked the door. I didn't like doing
it. I was getting a bad feeling about the whole thing. So I stayed
in the area and kept an eye on the hangar until I saw Blyleven's
car drive up."

"Are you sure it was his car?"

"I recognized it, yeah. A white Honda Accord. Anyway, Blyleven and another guy got out of the car, and I drove away."

"Another guy? Who was it?"

"I don't know, I was too far away to see."

"What did he look like?"

"I told you," he said, turning toward me, "I was too far away."

"Was he short or tall? Skinny or fat? Young or old? White,
black, or brown?"

"Goddammit, what did I just say?"

"Right. But you're certain one of them was Blyleven?"

He frowned. "I assumed it was him. Same car, same general
build. Besides, this whole thing was his plan."

"Did you see them take anything out of the car?"

"No. I drove away, went back to my rounds. At midnight I
returned to the hangar. The two guys and the car were gone, so I
locked up. That was that. The next day, I waited to hear how the
big surprise had gone." He sucked in a deep breath and let it
out. "Of course, what I heard was that the plane had blown up
in midair."

"The feds questioned you about that night."

"They questioned everybody."

"And you didn't tell them any of this."

"What was I supposed to say? 'Sure, guys, I took a bribe,
I unlocked the hangar so Blyleven could go in there and plant
a bomb.' ''

"Then you think that's what he did."

"It's obvious, isn't it?" he said loudly. His face was flushed with anger and shame. "I've had to live with that every day for four years. If I would've told the feds back then, they would've locked me up and lost the key. They wanted somebody to take the blame, and I would've been it." He set his jaw. "But you know the worst thing?"

I waited.

"Blyleven *knew* all that. He conned me, got me to help him kill himself and Larry Foster, and he knew I'd never be able to tell anyone afterward. Unless I was prepared to share the blame and go to federal prison. Which I wasn't then, and I'm not now. An ex-cop in prison? I'd eat my gun first."

I said nothing. I was thinking about the people Blyleven had used. Earl Wilson, Larry Foster. His own wife. Who else, I wondered.

"So now you know everything," he said. "So now you can get the hell out of here and leave me alone."

"I'm sorry for you, Earl," I said. I meant it.

I left him staring down at his soiled gloves and trowel and trying to decide if he was still in the mood to weed his garden.

19

Back in Denver I stopped for a late lunch at a Mexican place on South Broadway. There were about a dozen tables with mismatched chairs, and all but three were empty. A mean-looking character with a drooping mustache and a straw cowboy hat was shoveling chili con carne in his mouth like he was one step ahead of the Federales, and a young couple in the corner were sharing beers and chips and salsa and meaningful smiles.

I ordered, and the meal arrived about four minutes later on a chipped plate. The steak was thin, but it was smothered in excellent green chili and the beer was cold. Two out of three ain't bad.

It was two-thirty when I got to my office—four-thirty in Washington, D.C. I phoned Mr. Lifkin to see if he'd dug up Blyleven's service record.

He had.

"Shall I fax it?"

Again with the fax. "You'll have to mail it, my machine's got a broken whatsis. Do you have his record there in front of you?"

"Yes."

"What sort of training did he have?"

"Hold on."

I could hear Lifkin shuffling papers. After what Earl Wilson had told me about Blyleven's midnight excursion into the hangar, it seemed pretty obvious that Blyleven had planted the bomb. And according to the FBI reports, it had been C-4. That was not something you cooked up in your basement with the aid of a manual. You had to steal it or buy it illegally—and you had to know how to handle it. In other words, you needed expert training. I suspected Blyleven had been schooled in demolitions or something similar. And it was likely he'd been through jump school, which would make it possible for him to bail out of the church's plane after it had departed from Denver. Assuming he was alive and—

"He was a clerk-typist."

"What?"

"He did basic training in Georgia," Lifkin said, "then spent two years at a base in Texas, where he made corporal, then two years in Europe, promoted to sergeant, shipped home and discharged."

"And all that time he was a clerk?"

"That's what his record shows."

So much for my expert-training theory. "Where in Europe was he stationed?"

"Frankfurt."

Germany. Blyleven and Stan Lessing had talked about Germany at the chess club. Swapping war stories?

"I'd like you to check on another service record for me," I said, and gave him Lessing's name.

"Middle initial?"

"I don't know. I don't know anything about him except that he might have been in the Army and stationed in Germany at the same time as Blyleven, maybe in the same unit. He's about Blyleven's age, and he's got scars on his face and neck from a bad burn. It could have happened before he joined the Army or after he was in."

"You mean, assuming he was in."

"Yes, assuming that."

"This may take some time. I'll call you when I have anything."

We rang off.

I checked my watch. A quarter to three. If I didn't hurry, I'd be late. I locked up the office and sped toward south Denver.

Cherry Hills Farm is on the "wrong" side of University Boulevard. Wrong, if you're old money, because Cherry Hills Country

Club and the weathered mansions are west of the boulevard. On the east side are the million-dollar homes of the nouveau riche—which means *they* earned it, not their parents. They're just as snobbish and paranoid as the westsiders, though. I could tell by the six-foot stone wall that separated the area from the boulevard—and by the pair of security cops parked near the entrance in their shiny new Jeep Cherokees.

They watched my old Olds roll by with hardly a glance. Probably thought I was there to clean somebody's pool.

The Reverend Franklin Reed's residence was typical of those around him—a twenty-room monstrosity of wood, stone, and glass that managed to look old and new at the same time. It squatted on half an acre of landscaped lawn and bushes. There were trees, too, but not mature enough to matter. All in all, it looked as if the God business was paying off.

I left the Olds in the circular drive, walked up to the wide oak front double door and rang the bell. I looked around for a cross or other religious symbols. There were none. Unless you counted the pillars that bracketed the porch, which probably would serve well for a good scourging.

When the door opened, I expected to be met by a house servant. But it was Reverend Reed himself.

He blessed me with a smile and said, "Good afternoon, Mr. Lomax. You're precisely on time." The words rolled out smooth and rounded with the faintest shade of a Southern accent. "Won't you come in?"

Except for a glimpse of him at his church on Monday, I'd only seen Reed on television. He seemed shorter up close, perhaps five six, one-forty. His curly gray hair was long and perfectly coiffured. He wore a white linen jacket, white silk shirt, white tie with a faint silver pattern, creased white pants, and cream-colored Italian shoes. His face and hands were tanned—his left less so than his right. A golfer. The only jewelry he wore was a simple gold wedding band.

He gave my hand a quick, firm shake, and ushered me in.

The foyer was no bigger than a ballroom and air-conditioned cool. There was an enormous oil painting on one wall depicting Jesus, dressed in white like Reed, ascending into heaven, while a handful of the faithful stood below, faces upturned in awe and adoration. One of them looked surprisingly like Reed himself.

"Interesting painting."

"Thank you," he said, admiring it for the thousandth time.

"Commissioned?"

"Why, yes. How did you know?"

"Just a hunch."

He gave me the briefest of frowns, then replaced it with a beatific smile and extended his arm. "This way, if you please," he said. "We were just sitting down in the garden room when you rang."

"We?"

"I've asked Matthew Styles to join us. We both appreciate your cooperation in coming here." Cooperation. As if this meeting were his idea, not mine.

I followed him through the foyer and down a hallway wide and long enough for a pair of bowling lanes. We passed a doorway on the left that opened into an expansive room with a stone fireplace and a huge bay window. There were enough sofas and chairs scattered about to fill a furniture showroom. Farther down the hall on the right was a room with a hardwood floor, bare walls, and no furniture at all save for a baby grand piano. It looked like an exotic black beast, captured and put on display.

Reed led me into what he had called the garden room. Aptly named.

Matthew Styles was standing beside a round white wrought-iron table. He was dressed as if he'd just come from an alumni meeting—navy-blue blazer, tan pants, striped tie. He nodded hello to me, then looked toward Reed for further instructions.

"Let's all sit down, shall we?"

The room gave the impression of being outdoors. One wall was entirely glass—that is, the bottom half was glass, the upper half a screen. It looked out onto an elaborate garden with miniature hills and valleys covered with a gaudy display of flowers. There was a gurgling fountain, several half-size statues of Jesus and a few of His close friends, and a meandering gravel path. Within the room were flowers in floor stands and hanging baskets, as if the garden were encroaching on the house. The scent was sweet enough to gag a bee.

"I often come here when I am of a troubled mind," Reed said. He sat far enough from the table to cross one knee over the other. I saw that his all-white ensemble was marred by electric blue socks, which stood out like sins on the soul of a saint. "It helps me to think."

"Hey, whatever works."

He held out his hand to Styles. "Matthew?"

There was a Manila folder on the table at Styles's elbow. He handed it to his boss. Reed made a big show of retrieving frameless half-spectacles from his coat pocket and placing them on his nose, as if he were on camera, about to deliver a sermon.

"We did a little checking on you," Reed said, opening the folder before him.

"I'm flattered."

"First of all, you couldn't have been hired by, let's see . . ." He put his finger on the open page. ". . . Fidelity Life of Ontario, as you told Mr. Styles. No such company exists."

"Did I say Ontario? I mean Ottawa."

"Really, Mr. Lomax." His tone was designed to inspire guilt. It almost worked. This guy was pretty good. "Who are you working for?" he wanted to know.

"My client requests anonymity."

He gave me a long, hard stare. Then he went back to his report. "Graduated University of Colorado, worked sporadically, joined Denver police department eleven years ago, married Katherine Webster three years later, widowed three years after that, quit the police, became a drunk, became a private investigator." He peered at me over the tops of his glasses. "Do I have it correctly?"

"You work pretty fast."

He took off his specs and tapped them on the folder. "It also says here that not too long ago, in a case involving the theft of a large, bloodred stone, you were charged with second-degree murder."

"The charges were dropped."

"Still."

"What's your point?"

"Just this, sir," he said, filling the room with his pear-shaped tones. "You are obviously a man without Christian values, a liar, a drunk, perhaps even a thief and a murderer, and you come to my church, the house of *God*, making veiled threats to members of my staff and—"

"I don't remember making any threats."

"I call it a threat when someone bandies out the name of a known gangster."

"Joseph Scolla."

"Yes."

"By the way, how long have you and Scolla been pals?"

He glared at me. "I deeply resent that. I had never even *heard* of the man before Matthew described him to me today. A member of organized crime in Arizona. A soldier of Satan. And it wouldn't surprise me if you were connected with him in some fashion."

"Don't make me laugh."

"Are you saying you're not connected with Joseph Scolla in any way?"

"You know I'm not."

Styles and Reed exchanged a quick glance. Reed looked relieved. Had he actually been worried that I was working for Scolla?

"What frightens you about Scolla?" I asked him.

He gave me a confident smile. "When you put your trust in Jesus, you have nothing to fear."

"Sure. Let's talk about Martin Blyleven. Scolla sent someone to Denver looking for him. Why, do you suppose?"

"I have no idea. Particularly since Martin Blyleven has been dead for four years."

Now I gave him *my* confident smile—although it wasn't quite as white as his. "What if he's alive?"

"Is he?"

Reed and Styles were watching me closely, hoping I'd betray some hidden truth. I made it easy for them.

"I honestly don't know. But I think he may be."

"Where is he then?" Styles blurted. "And why—"

Reed raised his hand with the last two fingers curled down, as if he were bestowing a blessing. It shut Styles up.

Reed asked quietly, "Why do you think Martin Blyleven may be alive? Have you seen him?"

"Let's just say I've heard from someone who claims to be Blyleven. And he knows things that only Blyleven could know."

"Such as?" Reed tried to act as if he couldn't care less. He cared, all right. The tiny muscles around his eyes were tight enough to make him squint.

"This and that," I said, making him sweat. "Tell me, why would Blyleven want to fake his own death?"

"I'm sure I wouldn't know," Reed said.

"Was he running away from Scolla?"

Reed shrugged and shook his head. No comment from Styles.

"Had he been *dealing* with Scolla?"

Same answer. Although Styles swallowed, bobbing the knot in his tie.

I said, "If you'll pardon the vernacular, Reverend, let's cut the bullshit. I think we both want the same thing here. To find out if Blyleven is alive. And if he is alive, we both want to know where he's been for four years and why he chose now to return."

Reed and Styles said nothing.

"Look, I know things that you don't know, and vice versa. Maybe if we pool our information, we can find Blyleven. Assuming he's alive. But we'd better do it fast, before Scolla's hired killer gets to him, if we want him to *stay* alive."

"Who says we want him—" Styles stopped himself short.

I smiled and finished his sentence. "To stay alive?"

Reed pushed back from the table and stood. He looked down on me from a great height. "This conversation is over, Mr. Lomax."

"Just when things were getting good."

"I trust you can find your way out. And if you ever come to my house or my church again, I'll have you arrested."

"For what, being an agnostic?"

"Get out."

I did, walking through the cool, spacious house into bright sunshine.

Obviously, Reed and Styles knew a hell of a lot more than they were telling. I didn't see how I could make them talk. They presented too strong a front. Together, that is. But what if I could get between them, somehow turn one against the other? It was something to think about.

One thing was certain—Reed and Styles both wished that Blyleven were dead. Of course, so did Manny, Joey the Jap Scolla, and Roger and Vivian Armis.

In a way, so did I. It would make everyone's life simpler.

20

At five-thirty, I phoned Nora Foster from my apartment.

"I got your message about Blyleven's briefcase," I said. "And there are a few other things I want to discuss."

"Oh. Well, I just walked in the door from work."

"Shall I call back later?

"Why don't you come over, say in an hour. You can eat with us."

"I don't want to impose."

"Believe me, throwing another burger on the grill is no imposition. You could bring some beer."

I got to the house at six-thirty. I'd changed into lightweight slacks and a sport shirt, and I'd bought a six-pack of Molson and a six-pack of Pepsi on the way over. I left my jacket on the backseat and my gun in the glove compartment.

I'd been wanting to speak to Nora Foster since yesterday's talk with Vivian Armis. And the thought made me a little sick. Vivian had told me that Lawrence Foster and Blyleven had gone on a two-day road trip prior to the plane crash. No doubt the two events were related. Which meant that Foster had been a willing member of the conspiracy that killed him.

Before I heard about the trip, I'd believed that Foster was an innocent victim. I had hoped he was. For Nora's sake.

Brian Foster answered the door when I rang.

He'd dressed for dinner—an Army green T-shirt large enough to fit *me*, purple jams that reached his shins, white socks, black unlaced hightops, and a baseball cap turned around backward. He frowned at me—or maybe my clothes. His white-faced golden retriever stood beside him, ears up, shaggy tail swinging.

"Hi, I'm Jake, remember me?"

He nodded. "Mom's in the back."

I followed him through the small living room and kitchen and out the back door, the dog at my heels.

Nora Foster was poking at coals in a round, red barbecue grill that had been wheeled to one end of the deck. She wore thin-strapped sandals and baggy khaki shorts that nearly reached her knees. Her yellow sleeveless shirt set off the green in her eyes. She smiled, brushing a stand of auburn hair from her face with the back of her hand.

"Hi. The coals are just about ready."

"Good timing." I set the beer and Pepsi on the redwood table.

"I'll have one of those beers," she said. "If they're cold."

"They are." I pulled two bottles from the pack and twisted off the caps.

"Brian, honey, will you put the rest of those in the refrigerator?"

"Okay."

"The Pepsi's for you," I told him.

He wrinkled his brow in a small, thoughtful frown. "I probably won't drink this," he said, and scooped up the packs. "I like Coke." His dog followed him into the house.

Nora said, "Sorry about that."

"No problem. It's a matter of taste."

"No, it's just . . . he's so serious all the time. It's been four years since Larry . . . since his father died, and I'm still waiting for him to change back. He used to be such a happy little kid." Her eyes briefly lost their focus. She used to be happier, too.

We ate outside as the warm evening settled around us. Nora lighted a pair of candles in squat glass jars in the center of the table. Their flames wavered slowly, hypnotically, like lovers dancing. Somewhere nearby a lone robin chirped away the dying light.

"That was excellent," I said. "The salad, too."

"Thanks."

"Mom, can I go in?"

"Sure, honey. Help me carry some of this."

I started to get up.

"No, please, stay here. It'll just take a minute. Would you like another beer?"

"Sure."

A few minutes later, she came outside carrying a pair of bottles, set them down, then settled into her chair, a quarter-circle around the table from me. She stared off into the darkness. The candles spread warm yellow highlights on her smooth cheek and upraised chin.

"It's a beautiful night," she said.

"Yes."

Even through the city's glow, you could see a lot of stars. I waited for her to return to earth. Finally, she sighed and turned toward me.

"You said you remembered something about Martin Blyleven's briefcase," I said.

She nodded. "I was thinking that Larry had said the case was unusual. But it wasn't that. It was how Blyleven *treated* the case. As if his life depended on it."

"What do you mean?"

"Larry said there was more than enough room for their luggage in compartments behind the rear seats, but Blyleven never put his briefcase there. The first time Larry tried to take it from him, he practically dislocated Larry's arm yanking it away. He held on to it during the entire flight, either on his lap or on the floor between his legs."

"Did your husband ever see what was inside?"

"No."

"Did Blyleven ever hint at what it might be?"

"No. But Larry said he was probably smuggling dope." She smiled when she said it.

"Why is that funny?"

She looked at me as if I were stupid. "He was joking. They were flying to Tucson on *church* business."

"Right. Did you and your husband go to church often?"

She continued to look at me in an odd way, the candlelight flickering in her eyes. "What's that got to do with anything?"

"Just curious."

She hesitated, then gave a small shrug. "I stopped going to church after high school." She picked up her bottle and took a small sip.

"Was there anything else Larry told you about the briefcase?"

"Not that I remember?"

"You said it was leather."

"Yes, brown leather, I think Larry said. Just an average briefcase. Except that Blyleven acted as if it contained military secrets."

"Down and back?"

"Excuse me?"

"Did he treat the case the same way flying to Tucson as he did when they flew back to Denver?" Maybe he *was* carrying drugs, one direction or the other.

"I really can't say."

"You're sure."

"Yes. Sorry."

"It's okay." I drank some beer, gathering the resolve to toss mud on her dear, departed husband. "On their final flight, they left around four-thirty in the afternoon, true?"

"Yes, I—" Her voice caught, and she cleared her throat. "Yes, that's right."

"Did they always leave at that time?"

"No, it varied. Sometimes it was in the morning. Although . . ." She frowned.

"What?"

"It was rare for them to leave so late. I remember Larry saying they wouldn't reach Tucson until well after dark."

"Was that a problem? I mean, as far as Larry's flying abilities."

She shook her head. "No."

"Who decided what time they took off?"

"Blyleven. He'd phone Larry a day or so beforehand and tell him when he wanted to leave."

"Always?"

"Yes."

"So your husband never had a say about that."

"No," she said, frowning at me. "What are you getting at?"

"Just trying to straighten it out in my mind. On the night before their final flight, can you tell me what happened?"

She was still frowning, but her eyes had come unfocused. She blinked and looked away. "What do you mean?"

"Do you remember the night before that flight?"

Now she turned to me with one corner of her mouth raised. When she spoke, there was bitterness in her voice. "Do I remember the last night I ever spent with my husband? The father of my only child? Yes, you might say I *remember* it." She snorted with disgust and stood abruptly. I thought she was going to tell me to leave. But she turned away, took three steps to the edge of the deck, and stared out at the night, arms folded, shoulders painfully hunched. Nice going, Lomax.

I watched her for a few minutes. She shuddered once, and then her shoulders seemed to relax. She turned her head to the side, still keeping her back to me.

"We ate at a Japanese restaurant," she said without emotion, as if repeating lines she'd spoken to herself too often. "Larry loved sushi. I had grilled salmon, and Brian had shrimp. On the way home we stopped and rented a movie, an Indiana Jones, I'm not sure which one. Larry and I went to bed not too long after Brian. We . . . made love. In the morning, I kissed him good-bye and took Brian to school. And the day after that they told me he . . . was dead. Yes," she said with sarcasm and pain, "I remember it pretty well."

"Was Larry with you all night?"

She turned toward me and dropped her arms. "I just *told* you," she snapped.

"I'm sorry, I had to be certain. You see, Blyleven was at the hangar late that night, and someone was with him."

"Well, it wasn't my husband." Then her look changed. "What do you mean Blyleven was at the hangar? What was he doing there?"

"Good question." I wasn't going to repeat what Blyleven had told Earl Wilson—to surprise Foster. Some surprise.

Nora came back to the table and sat down, studying my face. "Could Blyleven have been putting a bomb on the plane?"

"It's possible."

"God*damn* him." There was venom in her voice.

"I said 'possible.' We can't be certain."

But she wasn't listening. "Most of the authorities suspected that Blyleven had brought the bomb on board. I refused to believe it, though, because it would have meant that *Larry* knew about it. And that was impossible."

"Why?"

"*Why?* Because Larry didn't want to die, that's why. He would never leave Brian and me."

"I'm not saying he would. But what if he was helping, not knowing exactly what Blyleven had planned."

She shook her head and gave me a half-smile. "That's ridiculous."

"Maybe not. He took a road trip with Blyleven less than a week before the crash, didn't he?"

She gave me a quizzical look. "No. What do you mean?"

"Wasn't your husband gone for a few days during that week?"

"No. He was never away overnight. Except when he flew to Tucson."

I didn't think she was lying. But somebody was. "Well, maybe he told you he was flying to Tucson that week."

She frowned and shook her head. "He hadn't flown there in a month."

"Look, Blyleven's widow told me that your husband showed up at their house during the week before the crash. He and Blyleven drove off in two cars with provisions for a long road trip. Blyleven returned two days later with his car covered in road grime, apparently from a long drive."

"Larry wasn't with him. He couldn't have been."

"She said he was."

"She's mistaken."

"I doubt it."

"Then she's lying."

It was possible. But why would she lie about that, after telling me everything else?

I drained off my beer. Nora didn't offer me another. I was out of questions, and we were beyond pleasant conversation.

"I should go. Thank you for dinner. And thank you being so cooperative."

She nodded, looking sad and a bit confused. I wanted to change that. But I didn't know how. I followed her into the house.

Brian was not in sight. I could see light falling from an open doorway at the far end of the short hall. At the near end there was a small table with a telephone. Half a dozen framed photos hung on the wall. Five of them pictured either Brian alone or Brian with his mother. The sixth showed Brian as a little boy standing with Nora and a smiling, square-jawed young man.

I hesitated. "Is this a picture of your husband?"

"Yes. It was taken a few months before the crash."

"Would you mind if I used your phone?"

I dug out my spiral notebook, flipped a few pages, and dialed a number. It rang three times before Vivian Armis answered.

I said, "I want you to think back to that two-day road trip your husband took with Lawrence Foster."

"What about it?"

"You told me that he introduced you to Foster then."

"That's correct."

"So you'd never met Foster before."

"No."

"Describe him to me."

"Well, let me think. He was about the same size and age as Martin. Brown hair, I believe."

I waited.

"And of course, his awful scar."

Bingo. "What sort of scar?"

Nora said beside me, "Larry didn't have any scars."

I nodded at her and said into the phone, "Describe it to me."

"He'd been severely burned," Vivian Armis said, "on his neck and chin. It was the sort of thing you try not to stare at, but you can't help yourself. Do you understand what I mean?"

"Perfectly. Thanks." I hung up.

"You were right," I said. "It wasn't your husband who took the road trip with Blyleven."

"Who was it?"

"A man named Stan Lessing."

21

On the way home from Nora Foster's house, I spotted someone following me.

I'd been lost in thought about Stan Lessing. He seemed to be the answer to two questions that had been haunting me. One, if Blyleven was alive, whose burned body parts had been in the wreckage? And two, how had Blyleven managed to get a body on the plane?

I believed now that the charred remains belonged to Stan Lessing. He'd gone on the road trip with Blyleven, and he'd no doubt been with Blyleven at the hangar on the night before the crash. Blyleven could have murdered him on the plane, then hidden his body, probably in the baggage compartment. That would explain why Blyleven had arrived at the airport so early the next day. He didn't want anyone checking out the inside of the aircraft, especially Lawrence Foster.

Naturally, this was only a theory. And it would collapse if Lessing were alive and well and—

And that's when I noticed I was being followed.

I was on Downing Street, a straight shot from the south end to the central part of town. Just before Washington Park I'd sped up to make it through a yellow-turning-red light on Louisiana. The guy behind me had been hanging back about a block. I say "guy," but all I could see were a pair of low, wide headlights and the sloping hood and windshield of a new black mid-size car, possibly a Lexus. He came roaring through the red light.

It's not unusual to see that around town. You barely make a light, feeling that it was a close call, maybe even feeling guilty for breaking a traffic law. But when you glance in the mirror you see one, two, sometimes three more cars coming through behind you.

That's what this guy did. I probably wouldn't have paid attention, except he immediately slowed down. He waited until I was a block ahead of him again, and then he matched my speed.

Manny?

My little finger throbbed. Even in the weak light I could see the thin black line that ran the length of my nail. I reached over to the glove compartment, slid the .38 from its holster, and set it on the seat beside me.

Two blocks later, I stopped for the light on Alameda. The black car pulled over to the curb a block behind me and waited. There were other cars on the street. They began to pile up at the light, two of them beside me in the left-turn lane.

The light changed to green. I made an illegal left turn, cutting off the two cars, getting the horn from one and the finger from the other. I sped west on Alameda for four blocks, then hung a right at Clarkson Street, just catching sight of the black car in my mirror, racing to catch up.

Once on Clarkson I pulled over and stopped.

The black car screeched around the corner. When the driver spotted me, he jammed on the brakes. And then he punched it, flying by.

It was a Lexus, all right, a shiny black coupe with smoky windows. I couldn't see who was driving. I pulled away from the curb and tried to catch him. A vain attempt. The aging Olds strained with the effort.

When the Lexus reached Speer Boulevard, I was two and a half blocks back, doing fifty.

Speer is six lanes wide, three on each side of Cherry Creek, and always flowing with traffic. The lights were red for the Lexus, but it barely slowed down. It dove through all six lanes amid a shrieking of brakes and a howling of horns.

No way would I follow that act.

I waited for the lights to turn, then crossed Speer. I was only a few blocks from my apartment.

Manny knew where I lived.

I cruised the neighborhood for a good half hour, looking for the black Lexus. No sign of it.

I parked a block from my building, then walked down the alley, the holster on my hip, my hand on the gun butt. Despite the city light, there were still a lot of deep shadows behind fences and hedges. I checked out every one.

Logically, I knew that if Manny had been following me, he'd been doing it in the hopes that I'd lead him to Blyleven. He had no reason to ambush me. Still, I had my gun drawn as I went through the back gate into Mrs. Finch's yard. I checked out the rear of the house and both shadowy sides before holstering my piece and walking around to the front.

Susan Hoffman's party was breaking up. I'd forgotten all about it. Just as well, because Mrs. Finch was doing the breaking.

I stood aside as a dozen young people filed out the front door, casting nervous looks over their shoulders, trailing the sweet scent of marijuana. Mrs. Finch was standing in the doorway to Susan's apartment, her back to the hallway, her fists on her hips. She was shouting. So was Susan.

"This is *my* apartment, and I'll have a party here anytime I want!"

"The devil you will, missy! This is my *house*, and I want you out of here tomorrow!"

"You can't throw me out, I just moved in!"

"If you're not gone by noon, I'll call the police!"

I was about to intervene and try to smooth things out when Sharon retorted, "My boyfriend will have something to say about that!"

Boyfriend? She'd never mentioned a *boy*friend.

Sigh.

The next day I started my search for Stan Lessing.

I tried the obvious places first: phone company, post office, Public Service. No record of him. The Denver phone book listed eight Lessings, and I called them all, connecting with six. None of them had ever heard of Stan.

I'd have to ask Big Brother. The government may not know everything about you, but they know enough. Fortunately for me, most of it is public information.

A good place to start is the Department of Motor Vehicles. On the drive out West Mississippi Avenue I kept one eye on the rearview mirror. No black Lexus. But I could sense Manny's presence. The Lexus was probably a rental, so Manny could be back there in another car. I doubted that he'd let me out of his sight. Not until he'd found Blyleven.

I spent a few hours at the DMV, needling and wheedling and waiting, before they gave me a copy of Stanford Wiley Lessing's Colorado driver's license.

He stared grimly at the camera, a brown-eyed, brown-haired man in his late twenties, listed as five ten, one sixty-five. His scar was prominently displayed. It covered half his chin and all of his neck, disappearing into his collar line—a puckered mass of livid, purplish-red tissue. Obviously, this was the man who'd played chess with Martin Blyleven and later taken a two-day road trip with him.

The big question: Was he still alive?

His license had expired two years ago and hadn't been renewed.

The reason *could* be that he was dead. Of course, there were other explanations. For instance, he'd moved to another state. Or else he'd simply forgotten to renew his license. Or he hadn't bothered to. Or he was unable to. This last reason might mean any number of things—loss of sight, for example. Or a prison sentence.

Stan's old mailing address was on the license, but it was a PO box. Besides, it had been defunct for at least one year—I'd already checked with the post office. And he'd left no forwarding address.

I wasn't finished at the DMV, though. They also keep records of vehicles owned.

There was nothing for the past three years, but four years ago Lessing had renewed the plates on a 1976 Pontiac Firebird. Five years ago he'd also renewed. And six years ago he'd bought the car. The record showed the purchase price ($1,700), the seller

(Skyway Motors on South Broadway in Englewood), and the buyer's address (the PO box on his driver's license).

It also listed the buyer's place of employment.

Bargain Tire Company was in Englewood on Hampden Avenue across from Cinderella City, which twenty years ago could boast being the largest indoor shopping mall west of the Mississippi River. If *boast* was the proper word. Now, though, it was worn around the edges, and two-thirds of the shops were vacant.

Still, there was a lot of shopper traffic in the area, and the tire place was bustling.

Most of the building was taken up by half a dozen bays, all occupied. Each car had its own blue-shirted attendant, who seemed in no hurry to change the tires. The vehicles' owners stood outside the open bay doors, looking on anxiously, while air ratchets whirred and growled like weapons from a fifties sci-fi movie.

There was a small waiting room crowded with four customers and all the amenities of home—tortuously molded plastic chairs, auto magazines with torn covers, and an out-of-order coffee machine. The guy behind the counter was a young Hispanic with a mustache and chin whiskers and a tiny gold earring in his left lobe. When I told him I wanted to speak to the manager, he gave me a bored look and said, "Is there a problem, sir?"

"I'm trying to find a guy who used to work here. Maybe he still does. Stan Lessing."

He hesitated, then said, "Just a minute," and disappeared through a back door.

When he returned, it was with a guy who *had* to be the boss, since he was the only employee wearing a tie—a narrow, dark number that went perfectly with his short-sleeved white shirt, pocket protector, and military haircut. He was about my age and putting on weight, spreading the spaces between a couple of lower shirt buttons. His forearms were muscular, so he'd probably worked his way up from tire-changer to supervisor. He said his name was Nordstrum.

I introduced myself and told him what line of work I was in. He decided we should talk in his office.

It was just about big enough for the two of us. Nordstrum

squeezed behind his massive, metal desk and I scrunched down in the wobbly visitor's chair. The desktop was a mess of order forms, catalogues, and promotional flyers, with more piled on the file cabinets in the corner. On the wall behind him was a poster-size calendar showing Miss Lug Nut leaning over the hood of a Corvette. She wore impossibly short cut-off jeans and a skimpy bikini top, and she held an air ratchet in a seductive manner, blowing across the end as if it were a smoking gun. It was last year's calendar. I guess Nordstrum was nostalgic.

"The name's familiar," he said. "Lessing."

I showed him the copy of Lessing's driver's license. It jogged his memory.

"Sure. The scar. I remember him now. An asshole."

"Oh?"

"Always bitching about something. Too much work, not enough pay, not enough days off, you name it. He acted like the world owed him something. When he shut up and worked, he wasn't too bad. But I finally fired him."

"Why?"

"He got in an argument with one of my other guys over some stupid little thing and he smacked him in the head with a tire iron. The guy had to go to the hospital for stitches."

"When was this?"

"Four, five years ago."

"Do you know where Lessing might be now?"

"Don't know, don't care. Like I said, he was an asshole."

"Would you still have his employee records or job application?"

"Probably." He made no move to get up.

"I was hoping not to go though the hassle of having my attorney subpoena them."

"Yeah, sure," he said wearily, and pushed out of his chair. He pawed through one of the file cabinets for a few minutes, finally pulling out a folder. He glanced into it, then tossed it on the desk.

"Help yourself."

There was a single sheet of paper in the folder: the job application. It was nearly blank. Name, social security number, PO box,

phone number. Lessing hadn't even listed his previous employment. I guess on-the-job training is enough for a tire changer.

I wrote down the phone number, not really expecting anything
from it.

"Any idea where he was living when he worked here?"

Nordstrum frowned, reached over, and took the file from me.
He scanned it, moving his lips. "A post office box. Wait. I seem
to recall he was living with his girlfriend."

"Do you remember her name?"

He smiled for the first time. "Yeah, as a matter of fact I do.
Debbie. Same as my wife."

"Last name?"

"Can't help you there."

I thanked him and got up to leave.

"Hold on, I've got something else for you." He rummaged
through a desk drawer for what I hoped was a better lead to
finding Stan Lessing. "Here you go." He handed me a small,
square sheet of pink paper with scrolled edges and a lot of fine
print.

"What's this?"

"Ten percent off your next tire rotation."

22

I drove back to the office to check my city directory for the phone number Nordstrum had given me.

There was a message on my machine.

"Jake, it's Hal Zimmerman. I found out a few things for you. Give me a call." He left his number and extension at the Phoenix paper.

Before I called him, though, I dialed up Lifkin Investigations in Washington, D.C. Lifkin's secretary told me that her boss was "in the field." I asked her to give him the full name of the man I was looking for: Stanford Wiley Lessing. That should cut down his search time. And his fee. I had an uneasy feeling that Lifkin charged top dollar. Not that *I'd* have to pay it. But I didn't like passing along outrageous expenses to my clients.

I phoned Hal, and he picked up on the first ring.

"I'll be brief," he said. "I'm already late for a meeting."

"Shoot."

"First of all, I could find no direct connection between Franklin Reed and any mob figures, including Joey the Jap Scolla and Manny Mancusso. But there are some indirect ties."

"Such as?"

"Reed's church owns a sizable retirement community in Tucson. It was built ten years ago, and the principal contractor was an outfit called Horizon Construction. A few years after the community was built, a federal investigation uncovered a number of mob-controlled companies in the Southwest. Horizon was one of them.''

''That's a pretty thin tie to Reed.''

''It gets better. Another business found to be controlled by the Mafia—and when I say 'Mafia in Tucson,' think Joey Scolla— was a resort hotel called The Palms. Ever heard of it?''

''No.''

''It turned out to be, if you'll pardon the pun, a hotbed of prostitution. Guests there could order everything they wanted from room service, and I do mean everything. The feds also found video cameras behind two-way mirrors in some of the rooms. And dozens of video tapes.''

''Are you telling me that Reverend Reed was taped in the act?''

''No. At least not on any of the tapes that were confiscated. But his name appeared on the guest register half a dozen times. The feds took all the records as part of their investigation, and they questioned hundreds of former guests, many of them public figures. Reed was one. According to the newspaper articles I found, he said he was visiting Tucson on church business. He professed complete innocence.''

''Who wouldn't?''

''The reporter asked him why he hadn't simply stayed in one of the church-owned condos. His reply: 'Because they were all occupied.' Which, according to the reporter, was not the case. You can draw your own conclusions.''

''When was this?''

''The bust?''

''No, Reed's visits.''

''They were spread out over a two-year period, ending six and a half years ago. That's the last time his name appeared on the hotel registry, anyway.''

I was trying to remember what Matthew Styles had told me last Monday. ''Isn't that about when World Flock went into operation?''

''Right. Six years ago. I did some checking on that, too. World Flock is considered part of the church, so there's no way to get a look at their records—which are tax-exempt and protected by

God, so to speak. Their offices are in the same complex as the retirement community. They accept donations to build and operate hospitals and orphanages in whatever country needs them the most. How they decide which countries, I don't know. Maybe throw a dart at a globe. As for dollar amounts, their ads claim they send 'millions to those in need.' Hold on a sec.'' He said something away from the phone. Then to me, "Jake, I've got to run. I hope some of this helps you out.''

He hung up before I could tell him it had.

Although I still didn't know why Martin Blyleven would want to fake his death. Or why everyone now wanted him dead. But I felt certain that the Church of the Nazarene and World Flock were deeply involved. I needed to know more about them, and I doubted that anyone presently employed by Reed would help me.

A former employee, though, might.

I flipped through my notebook for the name of the accountant who had been replaced by Martin Blyleven. Bill McPhee. There was a listing in the Denver phone book for a McPhee, Wm. I dialed his number. Ten rings and no answer.

Then I dug out the city directory and looked up the phone number I'd gotten from Stan Lessing's job application.

The directory has the same information as a phone book—name, address, and phone number. But it lists them differently. You can look up an address and find out who lives there and what their phone number is. Or, if all you have is the number, you can find out the person's name and address.

The number I had was listed to a D. Ogborn on Mosier Place in west Denver.

Stan's ex-boss told me that Lessing's girlfriend's name was Debbie. *D* for Debbie. Of course, the *D* could stand for Dagmar or Dashiell. My information was at least four years old, and people move.

I dialed the number and a man answered.

"What.''

I hate it when people do that. "May I speak to Debbie, please?''

"Who's this?''

I heard voices in the background that sounded like a TV. I also heard a small child crying, whom I believed to be real.

"My name is Jacob Lomax and—"

"Hey!" he shouted away from the phone. "Can't you shut that kid up?"

A woman's voice, low and unintelligible.

"Well, goddammit, do *something*. Some guy wants to talk to you named Lomax. Who is he?"

She said something I couldn't understand.

"How the fuck should *I* know what he wants. Do you know him or not?"

She said something else.

The guy said to me, "We never heard of you," and he hung up.

I startled to dial again, then stopped. A waste of time. At least I knew that someone named Debbie lived there. May as well drop by for a chat.

Before I left the office, I tried Bill McPhee's number again. Still no answer. I locked up and drove to the west side of town.

The late-afternoon sky was getting busy with clouds. Dark and heavy looking, they sailed over the mountains like purposeful spirits, summoned by the prayers of farmers on the eastern plains. Their breath was cool, and they rumbled as they moved.

I found Mosier Place, and parked behind a steely-gray GMC pickup with one taped brake light and no tailgate.

The street was a long string of tiny, worn-out frame houses. Debbie's address looked a little more worn than the others. The roof needed shingles, the exterior needed paint, and the lawn needed water. Windblown trash, empty soda cans, and a few child's toys festooned the yard. There were dark stains running down the sides of the front windows, like the tracks of old tears.

I had to step over a plastic tricycle on the stoop. The front door was closed, but it was thin enough to hear through. A man and a woman yelling at each other. I wondered if this was a new argument or a continuation of the one I'd heard on the phone fifteen minutes ago.

I knocked loudly, and the yelling stopped.

A moment later the door was yanked open. I was disappointed. I guess I'd been half expecting Stan Lessing. But this guy looked nothing like the photo on Lessing's driver's license. First of all, no scar. Secondly, no hair, at least on top. He'd let the side fringes grow long, though, and they hung in a shag that he'd tucked behind his ears. He was around forty, and his nose had been broken more than once. He wore grimy sneakers, baggy jeans, and a faded red T-shirt that was stretched tightly over his shoulders, biceps, and beer belly. He held the doorknob in one hand and a can of Coors in the other. Even through the dirty screen I could see he needed a shave.

"What."

The same way he answered the phone.

"I'm the one who just called. Jacob Lomax."

"What?" He managed to look confused and belligerent at the same time.

"I'm a private detective, and I'm looking for someone who Debbie might know. May I speak to her, please?"

"Who is it, Cliff?"

A blond woman in her mid-twenties with black roots and a sleeveless, lime-green blouse was trying to see around Cliff.

"Some guy," he said over his shoulder. Then he demanded from me, "Who're looking for?"

"Stan Lessing."

"Stan?" the woman said.

"Right. Are you Debbie Ogborn?"

"Yes, but—"

"So it's *Stan* now?" Cliff turned sideways so he could speak directly to Debbie and still keep an eye on me. "*Stan's* the guy you've been seeing?"

"I'm not seeing *anybody*, you dumb shit!" she yelled in his face. "How many times do I have to *say* it?"

"Then where the hell were you last night when—"

"I've told you *twenty times*. I had to work late because one of the other waitresses called in *sick*!"

"Then why didn't you tell me Stan was back in town?" he shouted. They both seemed oblivious to my presence.

"Because I didn't know it!"

"You lying bitch! You're seeing him again!"

"I'm not seeing *anybody*! Jesus Christ!"

He raised his hand as if to slap her. Then he sort of waved, shooing away the notion. "Ah, fuck it." He turned and stomped into the recesses of the house.

Debbie spoke confidentially to me: "God, sometimes he makes me so mad."

"I'm sorry if I caused a problem."

"Oh, *you* didn't." She glanced over her shoulder, then said, "See, Cliff moved in here about a year ago, and a few months later he lost his job. It's made him sort of edgy."

"Right. I take it you know Stan Lessing."

She pursed her lips and gave me a disgusted look. She had probably been pretty once, but life had knocked her around too much, leaving her with premature bags under her eyes, a permanent scowl, and an unemployed boyfriend fifteen years her senior. "Oh, I know Stan, all right. Is he back in town?"

"I don't know. I'm trying to find him."

"Good luck," she said sourly. "He got me pregnant four years ago, and then he made a big score and disappeared. I haven't seen that son of a bitch since."

"What do you mean, 'a big score'?"

She gave me a hard look, as if she were seeing me for the first time. "Who did you say you were?"

I told her, and showed her my ID to prove it. She opened the screen door to get a better look. There was a large bruise on her right biceps, blue and fading, days old.

"A private eye, huh?"

I put away my wallet. "Tell me about Stan's big score."

She looked me up and down and gave me a wry smile. "You might as well come in."

23

Debbie led me into a house choked with shabby furniture and smelling of last night's fried food. A little girl sat in the corner of the room in an enormous blue recliner. She wore a faded pink dress and sucked her thumb.

"Go on, sit down." Debbie waved me toward a couch with uneven seat cushions and dingy covers on the arms. She acted as if the little girl weren't there. "You want a beer or something?"

"No, thanks."

I could hear Cliff in the kitchen, slamming cupboard doors and cursing to himself.

I sat on the edge of the seat, glancing toward the kitchen doorway. This place brought back bad memories.

When I was a Denver cop, the most dreaded call we'd get was not "robbery in progress," or even "shots fired." Sure, those would get your blood pumping. But at least you had an idea of what you were heading into. No, the one that really put you on edge was "domestic dispute." Because anything could happen. You went into someone's home where the emotions were as white-hot and fragile as the filament in a light bulb. You'd put yourself between the two housemates, physically as well as symbolically. Sometimes they'd calm down almost at once, embarrassed that their private fight had turned public. They'd apologize to you and to each other. Maybe even hug and kiss. Other times, though, they'd join forces and turn their hostilities toward you. Come at you literally tooth and nail.

Once, when I was a rookie, my veteran partner and I interrupted a hell-raiser between a skinny little woman and her husband, a retired professional wrestler, three hundred and sixty pounds of fat and muscle. My partner did all the talking and got them settled down. They were contrite. They even asked us to stay for coffee. We declined. We turned to leave. Without warning, the little woman snatched up a steak knife and plunged it into my partner's back, missing his heart by an inch. A bit of residual anger letting itself out.

My partner recovered, but he was never the same.

So while I talked to Debbie, I kept an eye on the kitchen doorway.

"Let me guess why you're looking for Stan," she said. She was sitting on the arm of the couch farthest from me with her feet on the seat. Her black spandex shorts revealed a bruise on her thigh that matched the one on her arm. "He owes somebody money."

"Why would you think that?"

"Because he was always broke. He couldn't hold a job longer than a few months. Oh, he got a disability check once a month from the government, but that wasn't enough to cover his share of the food and rent. And if he wanted to get high, he'd borrow from me."

"Stan did drugs?"

"Just bud."

"What, beer?"

"No, silly, marijuana." She stopped and squinted at me. "Say, you're not a *real* cop are you?"

"No, more of a mock cop."

She grinned. "Mock cop. I like that."

"Did Stan smoke a lot of, ah, bud?"

"I wouldn't say a lot."

"But he did have a hard time holding a job."

She rolled her eyes. "Tell me about it. I'd nag his butt until he'd find work, and within a month or two or four he'd get in a big argument with somebody, usually with the boss, and he'd quit or get fired. Then he'd sit around the house for days, playing with his stupid chess set. Said it helped him think.''

"What were the arguments about?''

"Who knows? But Stan would find something. He has this *attitude* problem, like the world owes him something.'' She sighed and shook her head. "He never said as much, but I'm sure it had to do with his injury.''

"The burn?''

She nodded.

"How did it happen?''

"I don't know the details. Stan was touchy about it. Not embarrassed exactly, but defensive. Hell, I thought it looked sexy.''

At the word sexy, Cliff slammed a cupboard door in the kitchen. I sat up a little straighter. Debbie didn't seem to notice.

"All I know,'' she said, "is it happened when he was in the Army.''

"Where was he stationed?''

"He'd never give me a straight answer. I'd ask him that and he'd say, 'Wherever they needed me at the time.' ''

"What was his specialty, do you know?''

"Specialty?''

"What did he do?''

She gave me a wry smile. "He killed people.''

"What?''

"That's exactly what he said when I asked him what he did in the Army. 'I killed people.' I never asked him again.''

"How long were you and Stan together?''

"A couple of years.''

"How did you meet?''

"He used to come in this bar I was working at. An interesting guy to talk to, always full of big ideas.'' She smiled. "You might say he charmed the pants off me.''

Slam! from the kitchen.

"Were you married?''

"Naw. He just moved in here. Sort of like him.'' She nodded toward the doorway. "Of course, he *said* he would marry me, as soon as he made his big score. But then he took off. And that,'' she said, raising her chin toward the corner of the room, acknowledging her daughter for the first time, "is all he left me with."

The little girl had been deathly silent the entire time. Watching us. Sucking her thumb.

"Come here, baby," Debbie said.

The girl climbed down from the chair and hurried to the couch. She clung to her mother's leg, staring at me, her thumb securely in her mouth.

"Tell me about Stan's big score," I said.

"He was *always* talking about one damn scheme or another that was going to make him rich. Make *us* rich." She made a face and shook her head. "I should have believed him the last time though, because he was waving around cash. He'd never had any money before, just ideas."

"Where'd he get the money?"

"From his partner."

"Partner?"

"I don't remember his name. Some guy he used to play chess with."

"Martin Blyleven."

Her eyebrows went up. "Martin. Yeah, I think it was Martin. I don't know about the last name."

"Did you ever meet him?"

"No. He never came around here. Stan met with him every week for about two months before he ran out on me."

"On Tuesdays."

"Yeah, I think it was." She frowned with her eyes and smiled with her mouth. "Say, how'd you know that?"

"Lucky guess. Where did they meet?"

"I don't know."

"What were the meetings about?"

"Stan wouldn't say. He was real secretive about it, only that they were planning something big. When I asked him *how* big, he told me that his share—and *this* is why I figured the whole thing was bullshit—that his share was a million bucks. I mean, *seriously*."

"You said Martin gave Stan money. How much?"

"A couple thousand. But it wasn't all for Stan to keep. He had to buy some stuff for Martin."

"What sort of stuff?"

"I don't know what it was. Stan bought it from someone he used to know in the Army, and he kept it in the bedroom closet. He told me not to fuck with it, which was typical. My house, and he tells me what to do."

"But you saw it."

"Not exactly. It was in two black nylon backpacks. One was small, and the other was big with a lot of straps."

"Did Stan ever hint at what was in them?" I had a pretty good idea.

"Uh, uh. He said Martin swore him to secrecy. Oh, yeah, and something else. Stan gave him his car."

"What do you mean?"

She shrugged. "Just that. About a week before he ran out on me, he said he was taking a long trip with Martin. They were driving down to some small town in Arizona."

"Tucson?"

"No. Small. Someplace I never heard of before. Hole-something. Holman. Holton. Whatever. Anyway, Stan was gone for two days and when he came back, he didn't have his car. He said they'd *left* it down there. Can you believe that?"

I could. "How did he get home?"

"He said Martin dropped him off. I was at work at the time. He said I wasn't supposed to tell *anyone* about this. Like I'm going to go around bragging that my boyfriend just gave some guy his *car,* for Christ sake."

"What happened after Stan came back?"

"He hung around the house for the next few days. He was excited as hell. I knew he wanted to tell me what was going on, and I figured he would soon enough, so I didn't push him. He kept saying, 'Pretty soon we'll be home free.' " Her face darkened. "That lying son of a bitch. What he meant was pretty soon *he'd* be free. A few nights later I came home from work and found a note. It said: 'Don't wait up.' Very fucking funny, don't you think? That was his way of saying good-bye. He made his big score, all right. But he didn't need me to help him spend it."

"Did you ever hear from him after that?"

"Are you kidding? I never even heard his *name* until you showed up today."

"I see." There was nothing more for me here. I stood and said, "Thanks for your help."

She smiled. "Anytime." Then her mouth hardened into a grimace. "If you find Stan, be sure to tell him he's got a daughter now."

"Sure thing."

I walked out, and I had no sooner shut the screen door when Cliff shouted, "What the fuck was *that* all about?"

"It doesn't concern you."

"The hell it doesn't! I *live* here!"

"This is *my* house, you dumb shit!"

"Don't you call me a—"

I slammed the car door and started the engine.

Debbie was wrong about Stan. He never made his big score. Sure, he thought he was going to. A million bucks, Blyleven had told him. I wondered if that part were true. Of course, as far as Stan was concerned, the amount wouldn't matter. He was going to be an unwilling stand-in for Blyleven, a body to be used, blown to bits and burned beyond recognition.

And when Blyleven murdered Stan, he'd left another child fatherless. Mute, sucking her thumb, cowering, while Debbie and Cliff raged above her.

24

I found a convenience store on Mississippi Avenue and pulled
into the lot. It was just starting to rain—hard, fat drops plunging
from an angry sky.

There were a pair of pay phones outside, barely shielded by the
overhanging roof. Teenagers were not far off, for the outside of
the building was thick with their spoor—cake-and-creme smeared
cellophane wrappers, big-drink cups, and cigarette butts. I shoved
in a quarter and phoned Bill McPhee.

After I told him who I was and what I was doing, he said he'd
help if he could. He gave me directions to his home.

I drove through a hammering rain mixed with hail. It didn't let
up until I had exited I-225 in Aurora and found my way to the
retirement community of Heather Gardens.

The narrow lawn fronting the condo was white with hail.
Marble-size, no big deal. When they get as big as golf balls you
can worry. They'll pound dents in cars, smash windshields, and
rip holes in roofing shingles. Larger than that and you'd better
stay indoors. I know a woman who ran outside during a storm to
rescue her tomato plants, and she got bashed in the head by a fist-
size stone that knocked her down and opened a cut that took eight
stitches to close.

I called McPhee from the vestibule, and he buzzed me inside.

The elevator, a retirement-home model, took ten minutes to lift me up to the third floor. A smooth, cautious, quiet ride, guaranteed not to cause heart palpitations or dizziness.

"I remember when Martin Blyleven died," McPhee said. "Saw it in the obituaries. When you get to be my age, that's the first thing you read in the morning paper."

We faced each other across a low, glass-topped table with chrome legs. McPhee was cheerful and balding, and he sported a paunch beneath his powder blue sweat suit. He wore running shoes to give him better traction between the couch and the refrigerator.

His wife brought us coffee in yellow mugs. She was white-haired and bifocaled, and she, too, wore a sweat suit. Hers was pastel green.

"I can't say I knew him." McPhee said. "Only worked with him during my last few days there. But if he was anything like his brother-in-law Matthew Styles, he was probably a real son of a bitch."

"William," Mrs. McPhee said from the kitchen.

"Sorry, mama." He said to me in a lowered voice, "Styles was the phoniest bastard I ever met in my life. It always amazed me that Franklin Reed couldn't see through him."

"*Reverend* Reed, dear," Mrs. McPhee said, coming back into the room. She kissed her husband on his bald head. "I'm meeting Millie down in the gym for our aerobics class. There's more coffee if you want it. And cookies, too."

"What kind?"

"Macaroons."

"Macaroons give me gas."

"William."

"Well, they do."

She tsk-tsked at him, then smiled at me. "It was nice meeting you, Mr. Lomax. No, no, don't get up." She breezed out.

McPhee looked fondly after her. "A wonderful woman," he said. "Better than I deserve." He sipped his coffee. "But we were talking about Reed and the rest of them."

"How long did you work for Reed?"

"Twenty-six years. I was thirty-seven when I started. The company I'd been working for was breaking up, and I needed a job.

I papered most of Denver with copies of my resumé. The Church of the Nazarene was the last place I expected to end up.''

''Why is that?''

''Because I'm not a religious man. Never have been. My wife's got enough religion for the both of us. But Reed wasn't looking for another convert. What he needed was someone to straighten out his books. And I can tell you, they were in a royal mess. This was right after he'd been indicted for fraud, which you probably know about.''

''Yes.''

''Well, the first thing he told me to do was 'attenuate his culpability.' He actually used those words. In other words, cook the books and try to fool the auditors. I told him no way. He almost fired me on the spot. I explained to him that messing with the books would only get him in deeper trouble, and that considering his circumstances, honesty was the best policy. Those were *my* words. Honesty the best policy. Me telling him, the man of God.'' He shook his head in disgust. ''I could see from his ledgers that his church was a real money-maker. I told him that if he just hung in there, he'd be back on his feet in no time. Financially. Of course, his assistants had been saying the same thing, but I guess it took hearing it from an outsider, so to speak.''

''Was Matthew Styles there at the time?''

''No. He slithered in twelve or fourteen years later. And he's been running things ever since.''

''*He* runs things?''

McPhee gave me a wry grin. ''Everyone thinks that Reed is in charge. Probably even Reed. Well, he may be in the pulpit and on camera, but when it comes time to make an important decision, he asks Styles what to do. And then he does it. Believe me, I've seen it happen.''

''How did Styles gain control?''

''Reed let him. Styles may be a son of a bitch, but he's a sharp businessman. Even Reed is smart enough to know that. And to be honest, Styles is responsible for putting Reed on television and bringing in money from outside the community.''

''I see. And what about World Flock?''

McPhee snorted and stood up. "That phony outfit is what got me fired."

"Styles told me you retired."

"He and Reed *forced* me to retire. I call that being fired. You want some more coffee?"

He ambled into the kitchen and returned with filled cups and a plate of cookies.

"I don't know why she buys these things," he said, biting a macaroon in half and talking while he chewed. "She knows my stomach can't take them."

It looked like his stomach could take anything that didn't move. He stuffed the other half into his mouth. I pictured Mrs. McPhee downstairs in the gym huffing and sweating and waving her arms, while her husband sat on his butt and ate sweets. I sipped my coffee. What the hell. I had a cookie.

"You said you got fired because of World Flock."

"Because I asked too many questions about it," he said.

"What sort of questions?"

"Things I had to know to do my job. Like where all the money was coming from. I wanted receipts, check stubs, something. All I ever saw was stacks of cash and slips of paper with amounts written down by Styles."

"Stacks of cash?"

"Okay, let me back up. Normally the church gets its donations in personal checks, cash, and credit card accounts over the phone. They have employees who do nothing but count the money as it comes in and write down who gave how much. All very open and accurate. They have people watching the employees and people watching the watchers. 'To remove the chance for temptation,' as Reed used to say."

"But World Flock was different."

"You know it. Of course, I was there only at the beginning and then, boom, out the door."

"Tell me about that."

"Well, the whole thing was screwy to begin with. Reed and Styles had just come back from one of their trips to Tucson and—"

"Excuse me. How often did they go?"

"Styles went once a month to monitor the progress of the retirement community. Reed, not so often. Maybe three or four times a year. Anyway, when they came back this time I could tell something was wrong. I asked Styles about it, and he said I was imagining things."

"But you weren't."

"Hell, no. Reed was depressed, sick-looking, and he hardly spoke to anyone for the next few days. Styles was different, too. Nervous, anxious, as if something big was in the air. It turns out there was. World Flock. A week later, Styles explained it to me. He said Reed had a plan to gather money from all over the world and focus it in certain needy areas. World Flock would feed the hungry, minister to the sick, and shelter orphans. It sounded like an ambitious, worthwhile project. And I could see that it would take a lot of planning and organization to implement. But Styles said no. He said it was ready to go. In fact, he told me that World Flock would begin operation within the week."

"How did he manage that?"

"That's what I wanted to know. He told me not to worry about it, that all I had to do was keep the books." McPhee picked up a macaroon, then put it back down. "And the money started pouring in. I mean a *lot* of money."

"How much?"

"Half a million the first week alone. More after that."

"And this was all in cash?"

McPhee nodded, his mouth full, having succumbed to the macaroon. "Bags of it," he said. "Which in itself was not that unusual. The church was accustomed to receiving donations in cash. Although never in amounts so large. The oddest thing, though, at least to my mind, was how World Flock seemed to just appear out of thin air, a fully functioning entity."

"How did it operate?"

"Actually, it was little more than a clearing house. The money would come to the church in Denver, earmarked for World Flock. Then it would be transferred to the Tucson office for distribution to underdeveloped countries."

"How was the money transferred?"

He shrugged. "By wire, I assume."

"You assume? Didn't you know?"

He gave me a sour look. "When it came to World Flock, Styles showed me only what he wanted me to see. When I asked for more, he said it didn't concern me. When I *demanded* more, he fired me. Simple as that. Then he brought in his brother-in-law Blyleven to take over my job. Keeping it in the family, I suppose."

"Someone who wouldn't ask the wrong questions."

"That's how I see it."

"Why did World Flock have its office in Tucson and not in Denver?"

"Styles said that's the way Reed wanted it. Which to me meant that's how *Styles* wanted it."

"So the money came in from all over the world, in cash, then was transferred to Tucson."

"Right."

"Then what?"

"It paid for the overseas construction of hospitals, orphanages, and churches."

"Are you sure?"

"Sure I'm sure. I saw documentation that verified it."

"Was all the money accounted for?"

"Yes. All the money that came into Denver was used for the construction of those buildings."

"On paper."

"Well . . . yes. I never actually visited any of the sites."

"Did anyone from the church?"

"I'm sure someone did."

"But you don't know who."

"No. But listen, I know these things were built. I've seen the church's promotional messages on TV. Haven't you?"

I had. Still photographs of whitewashed buildings in the background and smiling, brown-faced kids in the foreground, kids with new shorts and shirts from Sears and dirty, calloused feet. A narrator promised that World Flock was helping thousands of children just like these.

I wondered if that were true.

25

After I left McPhee, I headed back to the office. There was a message on my machine from Lifkin, PI. I phoned him at once.

"My secretary told me you'd called with Stan Lessing's full name," he said.

"Good."

"Unfortunately, you were too late. I'd already done background checks on three different men named Stan Lessing, all of whom were in the Army.

"Oh."

"I'll have to charge you for all of it."

Big surprise. "Tell me about my Stan."

"Special Forces," he said. "Airborne Rangers. His outfit was apparently involved in a few clandestine missions in Afghanistan, back when there *was* an Afghanistan. The details are classified. It would take a lot more time to try to dig them out, and I can't guarantee results."

"That's not necessary. What else?"

"He received a medical discharge."

"Because of his burns?"

"Yes. He was on a training mission overseas. A fuel-storage tank exploded, killing three soldiers. Their bodies were so badly burned they had to be identified through dental records. A few other men were seriously injured, including Sergeant Stan Lessing.

He was burned on his arms, chest, and face. He spent a few months in a hospital in Germany until he had stabilized enough to be shipped to a burn treatment center in the States.''

"Where in Germany?"

"Frankfurt. There are some odds and ends here, if you'd like me to read them."

I'd heard enough. "Just put it in the mail."

"With your bill?"

"Right. With that."

After I hung up, I pawed through the bookcase until I found a US road atlas. Arizona filled one large page. Cities and towns were listed in alphabetical order along one side. I could find only one that fit Debbie Ogborn's description of "Hole-something." Holbrook. It was a small town on the edge of the Painted Desert, about a hundred miles north of the crash site. It was also on a more-or-less direct line between Denver and Tucson. By air. By road it would be a long day's drive, maybe fifteen hours. One day down and one day back.

I put away the atlas and phoned Roger Armis at his bank.

"The three of us need to talk," I said.

"What is it?" He was understandably anxious. "Have you determined if the blackmailer could be Martin?"

"We need to talk in person."

He was silent for a moment. "All right. Come to the house tonight at eight."

I got there at five after. It was a warm, soft night. The Armis house, like the others in the cul-de-sac, stared at the quiet street with yellow window-eyes. All the lawns were tinged blue-black by the arc light on the corner.

Roger Armis had aged in the two days since I'd seen him. His slacks and shirt both looked too large for him, as if he'd lost weight. His face was haggard and pale, and there were bruiselike smudges under his eyes. Maybe I was staring, because he turned away from me as he let me in.

"Please have a seat," he said, waving vaguely at the expensive, little-used furniture. "Vivian is just putting Chelsea to bed."

As he spoke, I glimpsed them walking past the doorway to the stairs. The little girl wore yellow shorts and a green shirt with some kind of cartoon animal, maybe a cat. She had a button nose and large eyes, and she stared at me as if I were a visitor from some strange and distant land. In a way, I was.

I sat on the same cherry-wood-legged, hard-cushioned, low-armed chair I'd occupied before. Its form barely served its function. Armis took the couch.

"What have you found out?"

"We should wait for your wife."

"Yes, yes, of course."

We sat in awkward silence. What was there to talk about? *How was your day? Fine, hey, how about those Rockies?* In the room above I could hear the murmur of voices, adult and child. The words were unintelligible. The meaning, though, was clear.

I love you.

I love you, too.

A few minutes later, Vivian Armis entered the room. She wore cream-colored slacks and sandals and a dark blue silk blouse. Her hair was pulled back, and her neck was as long and white and vulnerable as a swan's.

"I'm sorry I kept you waiting," she said in a strained voice.

She settled gracefully on the couch beside her husband. Their fifteen-year difference in ages was never more apparent. Although she, too, had aged a bit. The lines at the corners of her eyes were more noticeable than before.

She asked me, "Have you determined if Martin is alive?"

"It's very likely."

"Thank God." She looked relieved. Armis, though, was pale.

"Why does that please you?" I asked her. "This man is trying to blackmail you. He's already put both of you through a tremendous amount of emotional strain."

She gave me a painful smile. "Don't you see? If Martin had killed himself, he'd be a murderer, because he would've killed Foster, as well. But if he's *alive*, then someone else must have blown up the plane. That's what he told me, you know." I could see she'd been spending a lot of time twisting this around until it fit correctly in her mind. She finished with, "I can live with a little blackmail."

"I'm afraid it's more than that. Martin Blyleven killed two people—Foster and a man named Stan Lessing."

"No," Vivian said, refusing to believe it. "You just said he was alive, so how could—"

"He is."

"Who's Stan Lessing?" Armis wanted to know.

I turned to Vivian. "You met him once, Mrs. Armis."

"I did?"

"At your home. Martin introduced him to you as Lawrence Foster on the morning before their two-day road trip. He was in the Army in Frankfurt, Germany, at about the same time as Martin. They may have met then. Or else they met at the chess club a few months before the plane crash, and Frankfurt was a point of common interest. Either way, Martin made Lessing his partner."

"What do you mean?" Armis asked.

"I should say 'consultant.' Lessing had been in Special Forces, so he knew how to handle explosives and how to parachute from a plane—two things that Martin needed to learn."

Vivian said, "Parachute? Are you saying that Martin bailed out of that plane?"

"Yes. After he killed Foster and Lessing and rigged the explosives to—"

"No!" Vivian's face had gone white. "You will stop saying that. I *knew* Martin. I was married to him for two years and he was *never* violent. He simply could not have murdered a man in cold blood."

"Two men," I said.

She stood abruptly. Her hands were curled into fragile fists at her sides. There was a pleading look in her eyes.

"He could not have murdered anyone," she said evenly, her voice low and tight. "There's simply no *reason* for it."

"Money."

"Do you mean the insurance?" Armis asked.

"No. I think he stole money from World Flock. Quite a lot, actually. Possibly in the millions."

Armis said, "Are you saying Martin stole from the *church*?"

"I'm not sure who the money belonged to," I said. "The Church of the Nazarene or the Mafia."

"The Mafia?" Vivian slowly sat down.

"They're tied together somehow by World Flock in Tucson. And I'm afraid your brother is involved, too, Mrs. Armis."

"Matthew?" She looked dazed.

"He makes the monthly trip to Tucson that Martin used to make. I think the purpose is to transport money."

She shook her head as if to clear it. "If Martin had been transporting money, he would have told me."

"He lied. He probably didn't trust you because you're honest."

"Of course he trusted me. He was my *husband*."

"Face it, Mrs. Armis, you never knew the real Martin Blyleven. He conned you."

We were silent for a moment.

Armis cleared his throat. "If he stole millions, as you say, then why is he back here trying to get money from us?"

"I don't know."

"And where has he been for four years?"

"I don't know that, either. Possibly, Mexico City. Maybe the two questions will answer each other."

Armis shook his head. "I still don't see how Martin could have managed all of this. You're saying he left a bomb on the plane and then simply bailed out?"

"I'm not saying it was simple. Lessing got the parachute for him and kept it at his girlfriend's house. He and Martin were together once a week for two months, probably so Lessing could teach him now to use a parachute and rig explosives."

"But if Martin bailed out of the plane, why didn't anyone see him?"

"He did it at night, or at least after sunset, in a remote desert area, probably within hiking distance of a small town—Holbrook, Arizona." I looked at Vivian. "Was he in good enough shape to walk ten miles over rough ground? Or twenty?"

"I . . . I don't know."

"Anyway, Holbrook is where they went on their two-day road trip. They left Lessing's car down there. It was probably stocked with a change of clothes, a disguise, phony ID, whatever Martin needed to get away. And start a new life."

Vivian's face was wrenched in pain. "It's impossible," she

said. "You can't live with someone for so long and not know who they are."

"It happens," I said.

Armis put his hand on Vivian's to tell her that it couldn't happen here. Then Vivian sucked in her breath, as if she'd just had a revelation.

She said to me, "Everything you've just told us is sheer speculation, isn't it? A theory."

"Right. But it's the only one that fits the facts."

"Maybe not," she said quickly. She chewed her lip, frowning, searching for the right words. "Maybe Lessing blew up the plane. He killed himself and Foster and—"

"Vivian."

"—and Martin was nowhere *near* the plane and—"

"Vivian, he boarded the plane."

"—and he's been hiding all these years, afraid to come back, afraid that *he'd* be blamed for it."

"Vivian, please." Armis reached for her hand.

She pulled it away. Her face had a slightly wild look, mouth twisted in a wretched grin, eyes wide and brimming with tears. "Don't you see?" she said. "Martin could be completely *innocent*." She turned to her husband and clutched at his hands. "Roger, he couldn't have done these things. He *couldn't* have. My God, he's Chelsea's . . . he *fathered* Chelsea."

As if that made him a saint.

Roger put his arms around her and soaked up some of her pain. There was plenty for everyone.

"We have to bring in the police," I said.

Armis nodded, stroking his wife's hair. "Yes, I'm sure you're right. We—"

"No." Nearly a wail.

Armis said, "Vivian, we have to. He's killed two people."

"He may *not* have," she said loudly, pushing away from him. "We don't know that for certain, do we?" She looked from me to Armis and back to me. "*Do* we?"

"Not for certain," I said.

"There." She stared at Armis. "We have to give him the benefit of the doubt. Until we know for certain."

"How can he be innocent, Vivian, if he's trying to extort money from us?"

"I don't know . . . He's desperate, he . . . he needs money and he's hiding." She looked at me. "You said the Mafia was somehow involved. Maybe he's hiding from them."

"It's possible, but—"

"There, you see?"

"But that doesn't mean he's innocent," I said.

She glared at me. "It doesn't mean he's guilty, either."

Around and around we go. I was tempted to pick up the phone right then and call the cops, tell them what I knew and let them deal with this situation and everyone involved.

Except that Vivian and Roger had put their trust in me. Besides, it was possible, if only remotely, that Vivian was right.

"What do you suggest we do?" I asked her without a trace of sarcasm.

She hesitated, licking her lips. "Martin said he'd call Monday and tell us where to bring the money. I'll ask him then to explain what happened and—"

"You asked him before," Armis said quietly.

"I'll demand, dammit! I'll *make* him tell me." Color had risen to her pale cheeks. She drew in a long breath and let it out. "I'm sorry," she said more calmly. "I'll make it clear to him that unless he explains in detail what happened, I won't give him the money. If he refuses, or if his explanation doesn't fit the facts as you've presented them, Mr. Lomax, then you may call in the police or do whatever you think is necessary."

I nodded. "You know, once he's caught, he may carry out his threat and implicate you."

"Let him," she said firmly. "If he's guilty of . . . murder, then he must be punished."

"True enough," I said. "But what if he makes you believe he's innocent?"

She hesitated. "If he *is* innocent of any wrongdoing, if he can somehow prove it to me, to us . . . then we have to help him. I have some money, and I'll give it to him."

"Vivian . . ."

"It has to be this way, Roger." She took his hand in hers. "Please."

He hesitated. Then he nodded. They both looked at me.

Great. "As long as I'm close by when Martin Blyleven tells his sad tale."

They agreed. I would return to their house early Monday morning and wait for Blyleven's call. That gave me three days to do what I had to do.

Vivian saw me to the door.

"You know," she said, after I'd stepped out onto the porch, "your entire theory about Martin is predicated on his stealing money from World Flock."

"That's true."

"And yet no official of the church, not my brother or Franklin Reed, ever told the police about any missing money."

"Also true."

"Then your theory won't hold."

"If, in fact, there was no money."

"How can you be sure there was?"

"I believe they'll tell me," I said.

"Why? I mean, why would they tell you now?"

"Because of the way I'll ask."

26

On Friday morning, I drove to Centennial Airport. The sky over
the hangars and control tower was so blue it looked as if you could
ring it like a bell. A tiny yellow aircraft climbed up there to try.

I found Thomas Doherty in the same hangar where I'd spoken
to him last Monday. His back was toward me, but I recognized
his mop of red hair and jug ears. He was on his knees, praying
before a biplane. When I approached him, I saw that he was
examining a greasy hunk of machined steel, one of several in a
metal tray on the floor.

"Good morning."

He turned and frowned. Then he remembered me. "Oh, hi."

"I can see that you're busy, but—"

"Look at this." Still on his knees, he held up the engine part
with both hands, as if it were an organ torn from a sacrificial
animal, its viscous lifeblood smeared on his hands and wrists.
"Cracked piston head," he said. "God knows how long she's
been flying with this."

I didn't know if he meant the plane or the pilot. "Can you give
me a few minutes?"

"Well . . ."

"It's important."

He hesitated, then reluctantly put down the piston. He got to
his feet and wiped his hands on a dirty rag.

163

"Do you still service the plane owned by the Church of the Nazarene?"

"Sure do."

"Do you know when it's scheduled to fly again?"

"Yeah, tomorrow."

That's what Matthew Styles had told me last Monday. Of course, he'd been known to lie.

"Who's flying?"

"Their regular pilot. Cal. He's taking Mr. Styles to Tucson."

"What time do they leave?"

"Cal told me to have it fueled up and ready to go by ten."

"Is that when they're taking off?"

"Well . . . no earlier than that. I can check. Cal may have already filed his flight plan."

"I'd appreciate it."

Doherty led me to his "office," a metal desk shoved in one corner of the hangar. He phoned the tower and asked about the church's plane. "Okay, thanks," he said, and hung up. "They're scheduled to take off at eleven."

"Which would put them in Tucson when?"

"In that aircraft? Around three-thirty, give or take."

"Where's the plane now?"

"In the next hangar."

"Can you show me?"

"Sure."

I followed Doherty outside, across a sunny expense of concrete, and into the adjacent hangar.

"That's it," he said.

He pointed to one of the four planes inside, the only one with twin engines. It was as bright and white as a blessed soul, but as sleek as temptation. I was pretty sure I'd recognize it when I saw it again. To make certain, though, I copied down the number stenciled on the tail.

"Do me a favor."

He frowned. "What."

"Don't tell Cal or Mr. Styles that I was here today."

"Why?"

"I want to surprise them in Tucson."

"Well . . ."

I gave him twenty bucks.

"Gotcha," he said.

I headed back to Denver.

I phoned the airlines from my office and booked a morning flight to Tucson. Plenty of available seats. Not too many sane people visit the desert in July.

Then I called Hal Zimmerman in Phoenix.

"You busy tomorrow?"

"I'm always busy," he said. "What's up?"

"I've got a job to do in Tucson that should interest you."

"Tell me."

I did. "I could do it alone," I said. "But it'd be a lot easier with two people."

"I'm in. I'll drive down and meet your plane. When do you arrive?"

"Eleven forty-five. Now as far as equipment, I—"

"Don't worry about that," he said. "I've got everything we need. I'll see you tomorrow."

I killed the rest of the day at the public library, whirring through newspapers on microfilm, reading everything I could find on Franklin Reed and the Church of the Nazarene and World Flock, looking for one more piece of ammunition. A waste of time.

I spent the evening doing something worthwhile—drinking beer at the ballpark.

The Padres were in town for a three-game series, and our home-boy Rockies had high hopes of catching them in the standings, since we were only two games behind. Of course, we were in last place. But what the hell, it's the beauty of the game that matters, the power and poetry of it, not the standings, not who wins or loses.

We lost.

On Saturday morning I packed a small bag, not really sure if I'd be away overnight. It all depended on Matthew Styles.

The flight was not what you'd call scenic. The mountains and plateaus that passed thirty thousand feet below me were as barren as satellite photos of the moon.

I thought about Martin Blyleven and Lawrence Foster flying this way once every month—much lower and slower, of course. Although I doubted that would have made the landscape appear any more inviting. I could picture Blyleven, peering down at the incredibly harsh environment and wondering what his chances might be.

Had he thought about the notorious D.B. Cooper? *He'd* made it, hadn't he? Taken a bag of cash and bailed out of a commercial airliner over the mountains in Washington. During a rainstorm, no less. And he'd gotten clean away.

That is, he was never seen again.

The feds liked to think that Mr. Cooper had died while attempting his outrageous crime. It kept their records tidy. Plus, they wouldn't have to waste any more time searching for him.

Of course, the might be right. Cooper might be dead.

And so might Blyleven.

We touched down at Tucson International right on time. I pulled my bag from the overhead compartment, and when I stepped from the plane into the passenger-loading bridge, I could feel the desert heat pushing in from all sides. There was a scattering of people waiting to meet relatives and friends. Hal Zimmerman stood out among them. He was a head taller than everyone else.

"Hey, Jake, good to see you."

"You, too, Hal."

He was about six six and one-seventy—a tall, skinny, middle-aged guy with a beak for a nose and a wide, infectious grin. He wore a billowy shirt, white cotton pants, and size eighteen canvas shoes. He gave me a bony handshake.

"Did you eat on the plane?"

"Not that I noticed."

"I need to talk to a guy first," he said, "and then we'll grab a bite. If you think we've got time."

"There's time."

We walked through the small, tidy, air-conditioned terminal, past baggage carousels and car rental counters to the office of the security chief. Hal knew him—a retired police lieutenant from Phoenix—and he filled him in on what we were doing. One, to get his help. And two, so we wouldn't get rousted by any airport cops.

"There's only one place where those small planes off-load," Roland said.

That was his name. Roland. A barrel-chested, red-faced man. He had a voice like a bear with the croup. He stood, wheezing, and pointed to a schematic on the wall. It showed the terminal, hangars, runways, and surrounding areas.

"Right here." He tapped the map with a thick finger. "No private vehicles allowed in there, so the passengers have to walk about a hundred yards to this parking lot. Unless, of course, it's a VIP."

"Then what?" I asked.

"If they've got a security pass, they can drive through this gate right up to the plane."

"Do they have to check with you beforehand?"

"Not unless it's somebody really big, where there might be a security problem, crowd control, something like that. Then the big shot, whoever he or she is, will let us know so we can make sure no one gets too close to them."

Hal thanked him, and we walked out to the car.

"Jesus Christ."

"What?"

"It's just a little warm," I said. In fact, the desert air had hit me like a blast furnace, drying out my nasal passages in one breath.

"Be glad it's not raining," he said.

"It rains here?"

"It pours. But it's late this year."

The sky was pale, with most of the blue cooked out of it. Mirage-puddles shimmered on the asphalt parking lot. The sun toasted the hairs on my arms and baked my shirt to my back before we made it to Hal's car. They say it's not the heat, it's the humidity. But when it's a hundred and twenty, believe me, it's the heat.

We drove with the windows up and the air conditioner going full blast. It helped a little.

Hal took us around the airport to the small parking area that Roland had shown us on his map. He pulled nose-up to a chain-link fence. There was an open gate to our left, wide enough to drive through. The sign beside it said, "Restricted Access. Authorized Personnel Only.'' Beyond the fence was a wide expanse of shimmering concrete, a row of hangars, and a few small planes baking in the sun. In the distance we could see an airliner gliding down onto the runway, then taxiing toward the terminal building.

"We could get some take-out food and eat it here while we wait," Hal said. "Or we could go get a decent meal."

I checked my watch. Twelve-fifteen. Styles and his pilot had been in the air for an hour or so. Doherty the mechanic had told me it was a four-and-a-half-hour flight.

"Let's go," I said.

We took Campbell Avenue north across I-10 and into South Tucson, which Hal explained was a community independent of Tucson, largely Hispanic, and with the best Mexican food in the state. We drove down a busy four-lane road, then turned up a narrow street. Hal stopped before an unassuming brick building. It had shuttered windows and a wooden porch.

Inside it was cool and dim. Coors had never tasted so good. Neither had chiles rellenos.

We were back at the chain-link fence at two-thirty. I was in the driver's seat, to give Hal freedom with his camera. It was an ancient Nikon, worn steel-shiny at the corners and fitted with a motor drive and a lens the size of a megaphone. He'd lent me a pair of 8 × 50 Zeiss binoculars, also worn.

We sat and breathed stale-smelling reconditioned air and watched planes land. Small planes. Big planes. Even a few military jets, which surprised me. But no sleek, white, twin-engine plane.

An hour passed.

Hal said, "Hey."

A black Lincoln limousine slid through the gate to our left. The windows were darkly tinted, and it was impossible to see who was inside. Hal exposed half a dozen frames, the camera's motor drive whirring, as the limo crossed a few hundred feet of concrete and parked in the shade of a hangar. No one got out.

"Is that our boy?"

"It's possible" I studied the limo through the binoculars. It sat as still and quiet as a hearse outside a funeral home, waiting for the guest of honor. It might have nothing to do with Styles.

Another hour passed with no white plane.

Styles was late. Had he been delayed taking off? Or had he postponed the trip? For all I knew he could have changed his mind and decided to fly tomorrow. Or next week. We'd have to wait and see. At least until Hal's car got low on gas. There was no way in hell we could sit out here with the air conditioner off.

Then I saw a snow-white aircraft glide from the sky like a dove. It settled into a perfect three-point landing. I could just make out the tail numbers through the binoculars.

"Our angel hath descended," I said.

27

The white twin-engine plane taxied toward the hangar. It slowed, then stopped.

The black limo slid smoothly from the shade, crossed the shimmering tarmac, and came to rest a dozen yards from the aircraft.

Hal's camera whirred and clicked.

The limo's driver climbed out. He looked more like a weight lifter than a chauffeur, a heavily muscled, slightly bowlegged character wearing ash-gray slacks and a black polo shirt buttoned tightly around his size-nineteen neck. He approached the plane from the rear, safely away from the still-turning props, and stood behind the wing. Hal and I watched his every move through our lenses.

"Do you recognize him?"

"I recognize his type," Hal said.

The passenger-side door of the plane swung up and Matthew Styles peered out. He and Muscles exchanged a wave. Then Styles turned his back to us and climbed down—awkwardly, because he clutched a briefcase in one hand. When Styles set foot on the ground, Muscles reached out—to shake hands, I thought. But it must have been to take the case, because Styles yanked it back and pointed up at the door. A guy in aviator shades, no doubt Cal the pilot, handed down a garment bag. Muscles took it, then led Styles to the limo and opened the rear passenger-side door for him. Before he closed it, I got a glimpse of Styles sitting with the briefcase in his lap, holding it with both hands. Muscles laid the garment bag in the trunk, then he climbed in behind the wheel. The limo swung around and headed toward the gate. The pilot was still in the plane.

I set aside the binoculars, put the car in gear, and followed the limo.

Once out of the airport we headed west on Valencia Road, then got on northbound I-19 and slipped into the flow of traffic. We merged with I-10 and sped by the tight cluster of buildings of downtown Tucson. They wavered in the heat. Or maybe it was my imagination.

"Joey Scolla lives in a canyon northeast of town," Hal said. He set aside his camera. "So we'll probably be getting off the freeway pretty soon."

And we did, following the limo off the Grant Road exit and heading east through town. I saw more palm trees than pedestrians. None of them looked too comfortable under the sun. The limo turned north at Kolb Road. Miles ahead lay some good-size, brown-flanked mountains, hazy in the heat.

"I'm surprised there are hills here," I said. "I thought Tucson was a flat desert."

"You know, they ski up there in the winter."

"You're kidding." Snow seemed a lifetime away.

The limo stayed on Kolb Road through a few twists and turns. Then a mile or so later it veered off onto a curving canyon road. Now there were no cars between us. Hal slowed and fell back. Between the trees that lined the side of the road I caught glimpses of a golf course, impossibly lush and green. But no golfers, not at this time of day.

"Scolla's place is around this next curve."

"You've been here before?"

"Once," Hal said. "A few years ago he granted me an interview. A state official had confessed to receiving a bribe from him, and Scolla wanted to give his side of the story. In other words, wide-eyed innocence followed by outrageous denial. But I never got past the front gate. I guess at the last minute he changed his mind."

"Why?"

"He didn't say. But a few days later the police found one of his bodyguards in the trunk of a stolen car at the airport."

"A gangland hit?"

"Or a domestic dispute. With these guys it's hard to tell the difference."

We rounded the curve. Up ahead, the limo slowed, then turned into a driveway. Hal drove past the driveway's entrance, pulled off the road, and parked on the shoulder.

"Let's go," he said, grabbing his camera.

When I pushed open the door, the desert heat rushed in like a huge, hungry beast, gulping our little bubble of cool air. I had to sprint to keep up with Hal, who ran in long, lopping strides—a *paparazzo,* eager to catch a celebrity with his pants down. I followed him up the driveway. The asphalt felt soft underfoot, and the white-hot sun scorched my bare neck and arms.

The driveway was barricaded by an iron gate thirty yards from the road. Twenty yards beyond the gate the asphalt circled a raised, landscaped arrangement of rocks and cactus that screened the center portion of the house. Although *house* was too modest a term for the sprawling, stark-white residence with arched windows and tiled roof. It was flanked by giant palm trees and fronted by a carpet of clipped grass.

As we reached the gate, the limo was just sliding out of sight around the landscaped mound.

Hal hustled off the driveway and jogged along the outside of the tall iron fence. I followed him over uneven ground, trying to avoid some of the nastier looking native vegetation. The house and the grounds were partially hidden by large, leafy trees on the inside of the fence. But Hal found an opening a few dozen yards from the driveway. He poked the lens through the iron bars, braced himself against the fence, and began whirring and clicking away.

The front of the house was fifty yards from where we stood. Through the binoculars, though, it looked as if I could reach out and tap Muscles on the shoulder.

He walked around the rear of the limo. The rear passenger-side door swung open and Matthew Styles climbed out.

A man was waiting to greet Styles on the wide, covered front porch of the house. He was in his sixties, short and chunky, with a deep tan and styled, steel-gray hair. He wore pale yellow slacks, white shoes, and an emerald-green silk shirt. His eyes were slightly slanted.

"Is that who I hope it is?"

"Joey the Jap Scolla," Hal said, his face still pressed to the back of the camera.

Scolla smiled, talking, and he and Styles shook hands. Then Styles handed Scolla the briefcase. They turned and walked into the house, Scolla letting Styles precede him and giving him a friendly pat on the back as he crossed the threshold. Meanwhile, Muscles was removing Styles's garment bag from the trunk of the limo. He took it into the house and closed the door.

Hal was grinning at me, rivulets of sweat tracking down the sides of his face.

"Tell me we're not good at this."

"Try lucky," I said.

"Well, maybe a little. If you want, we could stake out the house and see if they go anywhere tonight."

"I think we've got enough. Besides, I doubt they'll want to be seen together in public."

"That's a fact," he said. "Let's get this film developed."

"And maybe a beer. I'll buy."

Hal had already made arrangements with a custom photo lab in town for the use of a darkroom. Within a few hours we had selected a dozen of the most telling shots. Hal made two sets of eight-by-ten glossies—one for him, one for me. I told him to stay near his phone tomorrow.

I booked an evening flight back to Denver.

28

On Sunday morning after I shined my shoes, I put on a fresh white shirt, an understated silk tie, and my best summer suit (my only one). Then I headed off to church.

I drove south on University Boulevard, eventually flowing with the stream of cars that poured down into the lake bed-size parking lot of the Church of the Nazarene. I walked across the sunny grounds, merging with the host of worshippers who filed inside. Most of them carried Bibles or prayer books. As far as I could tell, I was the only one with a Manila envelope.

I sat in the back.

The pews filled rapidly. Hundreds of God-fearing folks, mostly families, mostly white, mostly financially secure. And most of them accustomed to being first in line. They'd expect no less when they got to the Pearly Gates.

We all waited quietly beneath the distant ceiling, bathed in brightly mottled light from the immense stained-glass windows.

Eventually, Reverend Franklin Reed appeared in the wings. He wore a purple-and-black cape over his business suit. The silence somehow became more profound. Reed strode across the dais and took his place behind the pulpit. I expected applause. There was none. Then I remembered where I was.

Reed began to speak—quietly at first, so that we all had to lean forward a bit and pay close attention. Which, of course, was the point. He got warmed up in a hurry, though, and I must say he put on quite a show, pacing the stage with a Bible in one hand and a microphone in the other, shouting, cajoling, raising his arms to heaven, leaning forward over those in the front row, speaking directly to individuals, and then to the entire congregation, pleading, nearly weeping, then laughing and rejoicing. We were cleansed. We were on fire, ready to do battle with Satan.

They passed the collection plate.

Whatever Reed said must have worked, because I felt guilty about not dropping anything in.

I remained seated while the crowd filed out. Then it was just me and the ushers. They let me walk all the way to the front of the church. But when I started around the dais toward the doorway where Reed had exited, someone behind me said, "Excuse me, sir."

The tall guy hurrying toward me was in his fifties with a severe haircut and a too-close shave. He wore a dark suit and Aqua Velva.

"Sir, you'll have to go out the way you came in."

"I need to speak to Reverend Reed."

"I'm sorry, sir, but you'll have to make arrangements with the office. Reverend Reed is preparing for the next service."

"I'm sure he'll want to see me," I said. "Please tell him that Mr. Lomax is carrying an important message from Tucson."

He looked at me uncertainly.

"I'll wait right here," I said.

A few other ushers had drifted over. My guy turned to them and spoke in a voice too low for me to hear, probably telling them to make sure this gentleman didn't attempt a sacrilege. I watched him disappear through the doorway.

Five minutes later, he was back, beckoning to me.

I followed him down a short hallway. He knocked on a door, then opened it without waiting for a reply. I went in. It was a small room with a desk, a couch long enough for a nap, and a few chairs. Franklin Reed scowled at me from his desk. On the wall behind him were framed diplomas and a simple wooden cross. His desktop was empty, except for a telephone and a legal pad, which probably held crib notes for his next performance.

"I thought I'd seen the last of you," he said.

"After today, you have."

"Then please be brief. My next sermon begins in thirty minutes."

"I'm not sure you want anyone else to hear this."

The usher was still standing behind me. He'd left the door open, in case he had to shout for reinforcements. Reed looked past me.

"All right, John, you can leave us."

John left.

I sat down.

"I didn't set out to pry into your affairs," I said. "It just turned out that way."

"What are you talking about?"

I opened the Manila envelope, withdrew the first black-and-white photo, and laid it on Reed's desk. He frowned at it—a shot of a man standing beside a limousine and another man looking out an airplane door. Then he recognized the man in the plane as Styles, and his eyes widened. But only for a second. He slipped on his scowl like a mask.

"What is this supposed to be?"

"Your right-hand man being greeted by the Sicilian Hospitality Committee."

I showed him the next few photos. Styles carrying the briefcase from the plane. Styles holding the case in his lap inside the limo. Muscles putting Styles's garment bag in the trunk. Reed's expression hardly changed, but I could see the wheels turning in his head.

"Why are you showing these to me?"

"Because they relate directly to Martin Blyleven."

Reed said nothing.

I said, "I think I've figured out most of what happened four years ago, how Blyleven blew up the plane and got away. What kept eluding me, though, was *why?* He wouldn't have gone to such extremes unless he had a very good reason. Yesterday, I found it." I reached over and tapped the photo of Styles holding the briefcase. "Money."

"What money?" Reed's voice was tight.

"Yours, the mob's, I'm not exactly sure. I was hoping you would tell me. Unless you'd rather I went public with these."

I spread out the remaining photos. Styles being greeted at the mansion by Scolla. The two shaking hands. Styles handing Scolla the briefcase. Scolla taking him into his house, hand on Styles's back. Muscles carrying in Styles's garment bag.

Reed sat back in his chair and gave me a superior look.

"These photographs mean nothing."

"There's a newspaper editor in Phoenix who would take exception to that."

He shrugged and shook his head. "I recognize Matthew Styles, of course. But as to *who* these other men are, or *where* these pictures were taken, or *when* they were taken, well, it's anybody's guess."

"Try Joseph Scolla and his bodyguard in Tucson yesterday. Trust me, Scolla looks just like his mug shots. And his residence is well known. As to the date, the license plate on the limo will narrow it down to this year."

"These pictures are of Matthew Styles, not me," he said calmly, giving it one more try. "*I'm* not responsible for what Matthew does in his spare time. Nor is the church."

"I think Styles will disagree. When the story hits the papers about a high church official consorting with a mafia *capo*, the members of your flock will come after Styles with stones and lit torches. Do you think he'll quietly disappear?"

Reed said nothing. His mouth was a thin white line.

"Of course," I said, "you know Styles better than I do. But I can guess what he'll do—try to save himself by turning against you. He'll point out that you're the man in charge. And whatever he did, he was only obeying your orders."

Reed swallowed with some difficulty.

"The news media will be on you like leeches," I said. "You and World Flock and Joseph Scolla. One way or another, the truth will come out. And my guess is, it won't be pretty. You'll be finished. Unless . . ." I paused to make him ask.

He did, in a small voice. "Unless what?"

"Unless *you* break the story. I have a feeling that Scolla, and possibly Styles, maneuvered you into World Flock. If that's true, you may be able to hang on to your church. You went through something like this years ago, as I recall, made your confession, shed a few tears on TV, and pretty soon you were back in business.''

"How could you possibly guarantee that I—"

"I can't guarantee anything," I said, cutting him off. "I'm merely pointing out your two options. One, you voluntarily come forward with the truth, well rehearsed and standing tall. Or two, you get dragged forward by the press, with Styles pushing you from behind." I gave him a moment to think about it. "But whichever option you choose, you have to do it before the story and those photos appear in the Phoenix newspapers."

He cleared his throat. "When?"

"Tomorrow. Unless this man hears from you today." I handed him a slip of paper with Hal Zimmerman's name and number. "But *I* need to know right now. Otherwise, I'll wait around here for Styles and let *him* explain those photos to me. And then to the press."

"And if I tell you?"

"Then I'm gone."

Reed hesitated. But I knew he'd already made up his mind. He began sliding the photos, one by one, into the Manila envelope. Then he put the envelope in his middle desk drawer and locked it. He sat back in his chair, hands across his belly, palms pressed together, fingers pointing outward, as if he were ready to pray.

"What do you want to know?"

"Everything," I said. "Starting with World Flock."

29

Reed told me that it started six years ago when, he was "lured into temptation" during a trip to Tucson. He'd gone there to minister to the residents of the church's retirement community, and he'd been introduced to a new file clerk named Jennifer.

"She was young and beautiful," Reed said sadly. "And I fell from grace with her."

Which might not have been so bad, except that they did their falling at The Palms, the resort hotel secretly owned and operated by Joseph Scolla. Most of the suites had video cameras hidden behind two-way mirrors. Before Reed knew it, he was being blackmailed.

"I should have suspected from the beginning that Matthew Styles was involved," Reed said.

"Why?"

"He's the one who'd hired Jennifer as a clerk."

"I see."

"But I was too distressed by the existence of those video tapes to think logically. They showed Jennifer and me in . . . well, let's just say that Jennifer was an adventuresome lover and the tapes were quite explicit." His face hardened. "Later, of course, I grew suspicious of Matthew. He worked hard to convince me to bow to Scolla's demands. And when I did, he made sure things ran smoothly. For Scolla."

"What were the demands?"

Reed shrugged. "World Flock. The video tapes of me and Jennifer would be made public unless I sanctioned World Flock. More than that, I had to sell the idea to the church council. Although, that wasn't too difficult, because the idea was a noble one—World Flock would be a clearing house for relief aid. Donations would be sent to the church earmarked for World Flock, then transferred to Tucson and distributed to underdeveloped countries."

"But it was all a phony."

"No," Reed said loudly. He took a breath and let it out. "Not completely. There were legitimate donations, and all of that money found its way to the needy. But . . ." He stared down at his hands, then folded them together. "But the bulk of the money that came through had nothing to do with the church. It belonged to the Mafia."

"You were laundering drug money?"

Reed gave me a distressed look. "Drugs, gambling, prostitution, I don't know where it all came from. I didn't *want* to know. It was delivered to the church as cash donations. Once a month it was flown down to Tucson on the church plane. After that, the money was 'paid' to bogus construction companies, which supposedly were building hospitals and orphanages."

He raised his eyes to mine. "I've tried every day to justify it in my mind. The church is *not* dealing in drugs or gambling or prostitution. We are *not* contributing to the profits of organized crime. And World Flock *is* doing some good." He winced and looked away. "But every day for six years I've felt as if I were sinking deeper into a pit. And I've been afraid to climb out . . . because of the video tapes. If they were ever released, well . . ." He looked at me and spread his hands. "The church would suffer great shame."

"You mean *you* would suffer shame."

He said nothing.

"How did Styles and Scolla get together in the first place?"

Reed sighed and said, "A few years before all this began, Matthew spent a lot of time in Tucson, overseeing construction of the retirement village. The main contractor was a company owned by Scolla. Of course, I didn't know it at the time. But I believe that's when Matthew and Scolla met and discussed the creation of World Flock.'' He smiled without mirth. ''Naturally, Matthew still likes to pretend that he's working for me, not Scolla. But he lives too well for the modest salary he receives from the church.''

''Unlike yourself.''

''I own nothing,'' Reed said passionately. ''My house, my cars, everything—it all belongs to the church.''

''Sure. Tell me, how did Martin Blyleven get involved?''

Reed's face flushed. ''I never liked that shifty little bas—'' He took a calming breath. ''Styles hired him. Our chief accountant, Bill McPhee, was asking too many questions. In other words, he was too honest. Matthew told me that Blyleven could be trusted because Blyleven was married to his sister.''

''I see. So once a month Blyleven carried cash from Denver to Tucson.''

''Yes.''

''Why?''

''What do you mean?''

''Why not deposit the money in a Denver bank and transfer it by wire?''

''Because that's not what Scolla wanted. According to Matthew, Scolla has strong ties to a bank in Arizona. That's where he wants the cash deposited—in an account set up for World Flock. By having it pass first through the church in Denver, it puts one more buffer between him and the money.''

''Who chose Blyleven as the courier?''

''Matthew. He made the first few deliveries himself, but after that he had Blyleven do it. The courier would be met at the airport and taken to Scolla's home, where the money would be counted. Scolla already knew exactly how much had been 'donated' to the church in Denver. God help the courier if the amounts didn't tally. That made Matthew very nervous. It's why he wanted someone else—Blyleven—to deliver the money.''

''How much money are we talking about?''

''It varied.''

''Give me a hint.''

Reed squirmed in his seat. ''Around two million. Sometimes more.''

"And this was every month?"

He nodded and looked away. "It still is."

"How much was Blyleven carrying on his last trip?"

"Three million, one hundred and seventy thousand. According to Styles and Scolla."

We sat for a few minutes in silence. Reed was staring down at his notes, wondering if he should stick to his original sermon. And I was wondering how Blyleven could go through three million dollars in four years.

"You and Scolla both put a lot of trust in Blyleven," I said. "And in Foster, too, for that matter. They could have flown off with the money any month they chose to."

Reed shook his head and smiled crookedly. "Foster was never a concern. He didn't know what was going on."

"And Blyleven?"

Reed looked pained. "Scolla had a meeting with Blyleven before his first trip. He promised Blyleven that if he ever stole from him, he would not only kill *him*, he would also kill his wife and daughter. Scolla said if they ran, he'd hunt them down like animals."

But Blyleven *had* run, abandoning his family.

"What did Scolla do after the plane blew up?"

"He was certain it had been done to cover up the theft of his money. He came to Denver. He *threatened* me. Right here in the *church*." Reed's face was flushed, whether from anger or embarrassment, I couldn't tell. "He accused me and Matthew of scheming against him. He had his thugs watching us and our families. And, I'm certain, the families of Blyleven and Foster. They were looking for the slightest sign that any of us had suddenly struck it rich or were preparing to run away. Of course, we were all blameless." He shrugged. "Weeks passed, and then months. Scolla had to accept the fact that the money was gone and Blyleven was dead, blown to bits. And that no one would ever know for sure what had happened."

"Scolla must have been suspicious when Blyleven's body couldn't be positively identified."

"Sure he was. Everyone was. But there was no way that the body could *not* be Blyleven."

"No money was recovered at the crash site. That must have told all of you something."

Reed shrugged. "With Blyleven and Foster both dead, we could see only two possibilities. One, a federal investigator had found the briefcase and decided to keep it for himself. Or two, the case is still out there somewhere, a crusty old leather bag stuffed with millions, lying in a cactus patch, waiting for a desert rat to stumble over it."

"So Scolla gave up on Blyleven and the money."

"He had to." Reed paused. "Until you came around acting as if Blyleven might be alive. Styles called Scolla and told him."

And Scolla sent Manny.

"What do you think Scolla will do when you come forward with all of this?"

Reed swallowed, looking ill. "He'll no doubt release the video tapes."

"Is that all?"

His face twisted. "Isn't that *enough*?"

"What I mean is, do you think he might try to hurt you? Physically."

Reed stared at me for a moment, considering the possibility. Then he shook his head. "No. Why should he? He'll simply find another way to launder his money. Attempting to harm me physically would gain him nothing. I think the video tapes will be sufficient revenge for him."

I thought so, too. Of course, there was still Styles. I said as much.

Reed's face set in hard lines. "I can handle Matthew Styles."

"Are you certain? I mean, for all these years he's—"

"That was then, Mr. Lomax, and this is now. He may have exercised some power over me when he was holding hands with Joseph Scolla. But Scolla will abandon him the moment I stand up and confess, of that I have no doubt." Reed's voice began to fill the room. "I created World Flock to do God's work, and Matthew Styles consorted with gangsters to defile it. They held my few indiscretions, my sins of the flesh, over my head like the sword of Damocles. But now I am ready to strip away the lies that have covered World Flock like a veil. I am ready to atone for my sins. And Matthew Styles must atone for his. Let us *both* be judged—by the congregation. And by God.''

"That should play well in the press.''

Franklin Reed nearly smiled. "You'd better believe it.''

30

I went home to change out of my church clothes. A cop car was parked at the curb.

There were a pair of uniforms standing in the front hall talking to Mrs. Finch. When she saw me walk in, she pointed a gnarly finger my way.

"That's him," she said. "And if he's in any sort of trouble, I want to know about it. I won't have troublemakers in my *house*!" She went into her apartment and slammed the door behind her.

"Are you Jacob Lomax?" the black cop asked.

He was the older of the two. I say *older*, although they were both younger than I—big guys with patient faces. The younger one had blond hair and a square jaw and looked like a college jock.

"That's me."

"Lieutenant Dalrymple wants to talk to you."

Dalrymple was no friend of mine. "He knows where I live," I said.

"If you won't come voluntarily, we're supposed to arrest you."

"For what?"

"Suspicion of murder."

I rode to police headquarters in the back of the cruiser and followed the two cops up the elevator to the homicide unit. Dalrymple was at his desk, reading reports. He was a beefy man with short pale hair and a wide freckled face. A thin white scar ran from his right ear, through his sideburn, and halfway across his muscled cheek. I'd been with him when he'd gotten it, years ago.

He told me to sit down and the two cops to take off.

We did.

"When's the last time you saw Jack Granger?" Dalrymple asked, not bothering to look up at me.

"Who?"

Now he did raise his eyes, giving me a stare that could burn away facial hair.

"Don't act stupid," he said. "You were in here last Tuesday filing robbery charges against three suspects. Detective Flannery showed you mug shots, and you identified one of them. Jack Granger."

"Oh, right. Him."

"When's the last time you saw him?"

"I'm trying to remember. Why do you ask?"

He kept staring at me. I swear I could feel a few stray whiskers ignite. Then he pawed through papers, dug out a photo, and flipped it on the desktop before me.

"That's why."

The photo showed Jack Granger sitting in a kitchen chair. Thankfully, his arms hung down at his sides—they weren't taped behind him the way I'd left him. His head was back and his mouth was open, as if he were surprised by what he saw on the ceiling. There was a round black hole in the center of his forehead.

"He was alive the last time I saw him," I said.

Dalrymple grunted. "What about this guy? Was he alive, too?"

He handed me another photograph, this one taken in what looked like Granger's living room. A large man was lying belly down on the floor. His head was turned to one side, surrounded by a dark stain on the carpet. There was a ragged hole in his face, just below the hairline. Shot from behind.

I could only guess what had happened. Jack had told Manny about my visit, and Manny had decided that his two hirelings were more trouble than they were worth. He'd killed Jack, then invited Wedge over and waited for him behind the front door.

"His name is Wedge. One of Granger's pals."

"His real name is Arthur Pool," Dalrymple said, taking the

picture away from me. "We've got a sheet on him. He and Granger were both shot with a nine millimeter. We didn't find the shell casings, so the shooter was probably a pro." He smiled without mirth. "You own a nine millimeter, don't you?"

"Nope. Only revolvers. Call me old-fashioned."

Dalrymple shrugged, and his shoulders moved under his shirt like a pair of bulldogs. "So you picked up a nine somewhere and ditched it after you popped Granger and Pool."

"Come on, Dalrymple. You don't believe that for a minute."

He raised his eyebrows in mock surprise. "Why not? They broke into your home and knocked you around, didn't they? And we both know what kind of guy you are. You wouldn't let something like that pass. So you came down here and conned Detective Flannery into showing you where Granger lived."

That much was true. I said nothing.

Dalrymple said, "Yesterday a neighbor kid peeked through the kitchen window, saw Granger, told his mother, and she called the cops. The coroner says Granger and Pool were killed sometime between Wednesday afternoon and Thursday morning. In other words, the day after you talked to Flannery." He leaned forward and folded his hands on his desk, crumpling a few papers underneath. "Fairly goddamn suspicious, wouldn't you agree?"

"You're probably right. I probably killed them both because they pissed me off."

He narrowed his eyes. "I want something out of you besides smart-ass remarks, or I'll book you for obstructing justice and lose the paperwork for a few days while your lawyer tries to bail you out."

I had no reason to doubt him.

"The guy you want is Anthony Mancusso."

Dalrymple looked smug, as if he'd frightened me into talking. But it wasn't him I was afraid of. It was Mancusso.

"Who's he?"

"He was with Granger and Wedge at my apartment. His friends call him Manny. He's a hit man, sent here from Tucson by a mob boss named Joseph Scolla. Check with the feds or the Arizona cops. I'm sure they can tell you all about him."

"What did they want with you?"

"It wasn't me they were after. It was someone named Blyleven, who supposedly stole money from Scolla. Mancusso thought I knew where Blyleven was. I don't."

"Who's Blyleven?"

I probably should have told him everything right then and there. This case had gone beyond the limits of my original contract with Roger and Vivian Armis. Still, I felt obligated to apprise them before I opened up to the cops. And Dalrymple hadn't exactly given me time to do so.

So I told him, "I haven't got the slightest idea. That's why I tracked down Granger, to get some answers. But all he could tell me is what I've just told you."

"Are you saying he simply invited you in for a friendly little chat?"

"Well . . . I may have burned a hole in his shoe."

"What?"

"It's a figure of speech. Anyway, I talked to him Tuesday night. And the next night I spotted someone following me. It was probably Mancusso, thinking I could lead him to Blyleven." I shrugged. "I don't know if he found him or not. As to why he popped Granger and Wedge, your guess is as good as mine. Maybe they were excess baggage. Or maybe they insulted him. You know how some of those Italians are."

Dalrymple was nodding his head. "Well, hey, I appreciate you coming in here and clearing all this up."

"My pleasure." I started to get up.

Dalrymple said, "There's just one thing I find a little hard to believe."

"What's that?"

"Your entire fucking story. Sit down."

I went over my story about a half dozen more times, telling—and not telling—basically the same things. Then I sat around for a few hours while Dalrymple dug up all the information he could on Anthony Mancusso and Joseph Scolla.

Manny had been in and out of reform schools and juvenile detention centers for the majority of his formative years. He did three years for armed robbery in his early twenties. That was the only time he'd spent in prison. Since then he'd been suspected of at least five gangland hits. Suspected, not charged. Lack of evidence.

Scolla had never been convicted of a felony. Although he spent his life wading through crime like a rat through garbage. He'd been brought to trial twice—once on extortion charges and once for murder. But both times the state's key witnesses backed out at the last minute.

Refreshed by this fascinating information, Dalrymple was ready to hear my story again.

And again.

He probably knew I was holding out on him, but at this point there wasn't much he could do about it.

It was late afternoon when I finally emerged from the police building. Where was my ride? Cops only take you one way.

I caught a cab home.

31

That evening I paid a visit to Roger and Vivian Armis. One more try. Blyleven was supposed to call tomorrow. That didn't leave much time to bring in the cops and the FBI—which is exactly what I wanted to do.

"Absolutely not," Vivian said.

The three of us were seated in their sterile living room. I could hear faint sounds coming from the rear of the house. Electronic *whoops* and *boings* and *whacka-whackas*. Chelsea watching cartoons.

I'd explained to them Blyleven's motive for blowing up the plane—namely, three million dollars and change. But Vivian refused to believe it. She'd been married to the man. She'd loved him. He'd helped her create a beautiful child. Ergo, he couldn't have killed *anyone*.

"Not for money," she said. "Or for any other reason. Besides, if he stole so much just a few years ago, why does he need money from me now? What happened to all those millions?"

"Maybe he lost big in the commodities market."

"Or maybe he never had it," Vivian said evenly.

I turned to Armis for assistance. He gave me a helpless look. It was Vivian's call.

"You know," I said to her, "I don't really need your permission to bring in the police."

"That's true," she said evenly. "But if you do, I'll refuse to cooperate with them. I'll deny that Martin ever called me, and I'll . . . warn him away."

I believed her.

She added, "I'm going to meet with him face-to-face, Mr. Lomax, and hear his explanation. With or without your help."

"He's murdered two people."

She pressed her lips together and said nothing. End of discussion.

"All right," I said. "I'll go along. But I can't guarantee your safety."

"Martin would never hurt me."

"I hope you're right."

We agreed that I would return to their house early the next morning and wait for Blyleven to call. When he did, Vivian would insist that they meet, just the two of them, and that she would give him the money. In fact, she had nearly twenty thousand dollars in cash that she was prepared to hand over—assuming that he explained everything to her satisfaction. And to mine. I'd be hiding in the backseat of her car, and I'd jump into their meeting at the first opportunity.

It was a half-assed scheme. But it was either that or let Vivian and Roger handle it on their own.

Back home, I opened a Moosehead and stepped out on the balcony.

It was a quiet evening, and pleasantly cool. Two stories below me and across the alley, one of the secretaries was doing laps in the small, lighted pool. Her boyfriend sat in a deck chair, drinking something with ice in it, watching her. The sky above was a deep blue, turning purple to the east. I didn't see any clouds. Behind me, though, to the west, I could hear distant thunder rumbling like freight cars over a trestle.

I stayed up for the evening news, watched Leno, then went to bed.

I dreamed of airplanes exploding in the sky.

One explosion awakened me. I sat up in bed, listening, telling myself it couldn't have been real. Suddenly, lightning lit up the room like a blue-white strobe. A second later, a crash of thunder.

I went back to sleep with the sound of rain thrumming on the balcony.

The morning was cool and cloudy. I put on a lightweight zippered jacket over my polo shirt—partly for warmth, but mostly to cover the .357 magnum in my shoulder holster. I didn't want any trouble from Blyleven. I hoped that *showing* him a gun would be enough. And the magnum was scarier looking than the little .38.

I drove west on Sixth Avenue. The sides of the road were still wet from last night's rain. Up ahead, gray and black clouds hung low over the mountains, acting as if they meant business.

No one was out and about in the Armis's cul-de-sac. Too early. All the daddies were getting dressed for work, and all the mommies were either doing the same or else trying to figure out how to keep Junior and Sissy and the twins occupied if it rained and forced them all inside.

I parked in the driveway and rang the bell. My stomach was growling. Maybe Vivian would fix us a nice breakfast.

Roger Armis opened the door and said, "Oh, hi," as if he were surprised to see me. He licked his lips and cleared his throat. "He called already."

"Blyleven?"

"Yes. He, ah, said there's a problem and he'll call back tomorrow."

"What sort of problem?"

"He . . . didn't say." Armis still had made no move to let me in. I tried to look past him. "Are you and Vivian all right?"

"Why, yes, of course."

"What's going on?"

His eyebrows went up and the corners of his mouth went down. "Nothing. I mean, it's just as I've said. You'll, ah, have to come back tomorrow."

I wasn't buying it. "Come on, Armis, something else is up. What is it?"

He gave me a weak smile. "Nothing, really."

Right. "Do you mind if I come in for a minute?"

"Uh, no. No, of course not."

He stood aside and let me in. I don't know what I expected to find inside—maybe Blyleven sitting on the sofa with a cup of coffee in one hand and some C-4 explosive in the other. But the living room was empty.

"What time did he call?"

Armis waved his hand vaguely. "About a half hour ago."

"A quarter to six?"

"Yes." He wouldn't face me directly. He folded and unfolded his arms, not sitting, not offering me a seat. He glanced toward the doorway, toward the kitchen.

"Who took the call?" I asked him.

"Ah, Vivian."

"Where is she now?"

"Upstairs. With Chelsea. She's feeling ill. Chelsea, that is." He folded his arms, then dropped them and put his hands in his pockets.

"What did Blyleven say? I mean, exactly."

"I already told you. He said he couldn't meet with us today, and that he'd call tomorrow."

"And he didn't say why?"

"No."

"What else?"

"Nothing."

"Didn't he ask about the money?"

"Well, yes, of course. He, ah, asked if we had it, and I told him, that is, Vivian told him that we did. He told her to, ah, put it in a flight bag and be ready to leave the house tomorrow morning when he called. Then he hung up."

"How did he sound?"

"What do you mean?"

"Happy, sad, angry, drunk, what?"

"Just . . . normal, I guess."

"Normal. I'd like to hear your wife's impression, if you don't mind."

He hesitated. "Yes, of course."

He left the room, and I heard him going up the stairs. Measured paces, in no hurry. I took a quick peek into the kitchen and the rec room. Both empty. Then I stood just around the corner from the stairwell and listened. I could hear Roger and Vivian talking, but I couldn't understand their words. A moment later they started down the stairs.

Vivian entered the living room ahead of her husband. She wore teal slacks and a matching cotton sweater with the sleeves pushed up. She looked pale, even haggard. Her daughter was sick.

"Good morning, Mr. Lomax." She managed a smile. Armis stood behind her and stared at the back of her head. "I'm sorry you made the trip for nothing. I phoned you right after Martin called here, but you must have already left."

"I must have," I said. "Tell me what was said."

"Well, he phoned at a quarter to six and asked me if I'd raised the money. I told him yes, that I'd packed it in a flight bag."

"How did he sound to you?"

"Pleased. He told me to be ready to leave the house tomorrow when he called. I asked him why we couldn't do it today. He said, 'Just be ready tomorrow.' Then he hung up." She folded her arms and gave a small shrug. "That was all. Then I called you."

I looked from her to Armis and back again. Armis kept his eyes averted. Vivian returned my gaze impassively.

I said, "I guess there's nothing we can do until tomorrow."

"Yes," Vivian said.

"I'll see you then."

Armis literally sprang forward and opened the door for me. The moment I stepped out, he closed it firmly behind me.

I drove out of the cul-de-sac, turned right on West Kentucky Drive, went up half a block, and made a U-turn. The only car parked on the street was a new blue Toyota Camry. I parked behind it. I could see a few houses on the cul-de-sac, but not the Armis house. However, I had a clear view of the T-intersection of the two streets. And it was the only way out.

I was certain that their story about Blyleven's call was a lie. If Armis's agitation wasn't enough to convince me, then his and Vivian's inconsistency was. Armis said Blyleven *told* Vivian to put the money in a flight bag, and Vivian said she'd told Blyleven that it was *already* in a flight bag.

I didn't know if Blyleven had called yet or not. But either way,

Roger and Vivian obviously had changed their minds and decided to leave me out. Probably Vivian's decision. Pay off Blyleven and ask him to go away. Never mind that he'd murdered Lawrence Foster and Stan Lessing. If he left them alone, they could forgive and forget.

I couldn't.

When they left to meet with Blyleven, I'd be close behind.

That is, if I didn't starve to death first.

I rummaged through the junk in the glove compartment looking for a forgotten Granola bar or a stray piece of candy. All I found was a dusty stick of spearmint gum that broke into a dozen pieces when I tried to chew it. It took me a while to meld it into its intended consistency. Of course, it did nothing for my hunger. But at least it distracted my saliva glands.

An hour later the first car emerged from the cul-de-sac.

The car didn't belong to the Armis's, though, just some poor working stiff in a white shirt and tie, heading for the daily grind. Too bad he didn't have a glamour job like mine. I shifted my butt in the seat and waited some more.

By eight-thirty I'd counted nine more vehicles coming out of the cul-de-sac: five men, three women, and one couple. No one had gone in.

At nine-thirty a Lakewood police car turned off Kipling Street and came down Kentucky toward me. He went by slowly, eyeing first the blue Camry and then the suspicious-looking guy hunched down in the old Olds.

At eleven the cop was back, this time approaching me from the rear. He stopped behind me, then sat there for a full five minutes. I could see him on the radio, no doubt calling in my license plate. Then he climbed out and approached my car.

Terrific. How come this never happens to stakeouts in the movies?

"May I see your driver's license, sir."

"Sure thing, officer."

He looked it over. "You don't live around here."

"No. I'm working."

His eyebrows went up.

I showed him something that said I was a private investigator.

"It's a matrimonial case," I explained. "A guy who lives down that street thinks his wife is cheating on him while he's at work. A nasty business all around."

He gave me a sour look, then handed back my ID as if it were unclean. "You people," he said. He nodded toward the Camry parked ahead of me. "Is that also part of your big investigation?"

"No, sir."

He wrote down the license number of the Camry and went back to his car to call it in. Then he drove off. I guess he wasn't used to seeing cars parked along here. After all, every house had a two-car garage. Why would anyone . . .

Stupid.

I suddenly knew why Roger and Vivian had been acting strangely.

I started to climb out.

Then a car emerged from the cul-de-sac, a year-old white Buick Le Sabre. Vivian Armis was behind the wheel. At first I thought her husband was with her. But then I saw that the man in the passenger seat wasn't Roger Armis.

It was Manny.

32

The white Buick turned left, and Vivian and Manny headed away from me.

I fired up the Olds, gave them a one-block head start, then swung out around the parked Camry and followed. The Buick went south on Kipling Street, which curved gently into Kipling Parkway. A mile or so later, Vivian barely made the light at Jewell Avenue and took a right, steering west toward the mountains. I stopped at the red, let a few cars get between us, then went after them.

I figured that Manny must have followed me to the Armis house last night. Then he'd parked his rented blue Camry around the corner and waited for me to leave.

Roger and Vivian were no match for him. They would have told him whatever he wanted to know. And he wouldn't have needed his toothpicks. Not with Chelsea there.

It was obvious to me now that he'd been upstairs with Chelsea and Vivian when Roger let me in. And when Vivian came down, Manny had stayed with the little girl. No way would Vivian or Roger risk trying to tip me off. Manny had been in complete control.

For that matter, he still was.

I wondered what he'd done with Chelsea and Roger. Had he killed them? Or perhaps he'd left them bound and gagged at the house, hostages used to control Vivian. I dearly wanted to believe that. But I feared that Manny wouldn't leave anyone behind who might possibly get free and call the cops.

I considered catching up to the Buick and running it off the road.

That would be the end of the situation. But it might also be the end of Vivian.

No, I'd have to wait for a better chance. Besides, they were leading me to Blyleven. Manny wanted him, and so did I. And if I had one advantage, it was that no one knew I was along for the ride.

We continued west on Jewell, a wide four-lane road that curved and dipped and rose between subdivisions, as the plains blended into the foothills. The peaks ahead were obscured by low-hanging clouds. Only the nearer hills were visible, still miles away.

The road narrowed to two lanes as it ventured beyond the frontier of houses. Nothing now but low, rolling green hills.

There were few cars. So when the Buick had to stop at the intersection of Highway 93, I hung back a hundred yards. Manny and Vivian had three choices now. Turn left toward the small town of Morrison. Turn right toward I-70 or Golden. Or go straight ahead into Red Rocks Park.

They went straight.

Fortunately for me, we weren't the only cars negotiating the twisting, rough asphalt strip that led into the mountain park. There were tourists in from the flatlands to see the pretty red rocks. And kids up from the city to screw around, maybe to try to scale the rocks—if they were dumb enough.

The snaking road cut its way through steep slopes, green with small trees and native grasses and freckled with purple and yellow wildflowers, bright even beneath the dark sky.

I heard a whippoorwill. I wondered if Vivian heard it, too. Probably not. She had other things on her mind—for instance, would she live through the day?

The road continued to rise. When it curved tightly to the right, I got my first sight of the amphitheater, half a mile away, huge red outcroppings of sandstone that jutted up from the green hillside. They'd been there for thousands of years. More recently,

someone had added seats and asked Yanni and The Grateful Dead
and Nine Inch Nails to fill them.

The Buick slowed at a fork in the road. To the left, I knew,
lay a cafe and souvenir shop and a vast parking area, both hidden
by outcroppings of rock. But the Buick went right, climbing
toward the rear of the amphitheater.

The road ascended, skirting the base of an enormous wave of
red rock, a wind-sculpted mass that flowed alongside the road,
then dropped over it. A square tunnel, just big enough for two
cars to squeeze into, was cut through the rock. When I emerged
from the tunnel, I saw the Buick climb the last stretch of road,
which ended above and behind the amphitheater at a small parking area.

The Buick stopped.

I pulled off the road and killed the engine. Sudden silence beneath a lowering sky. I heard distant thunder. Up ahead I could
see eight or ten cars parked in the lot. A few people milled around,
gawking at the huge walls of rock that defined the amphitheater.

Vivian climbed out of the Buick and moved stiffly to the front
bumper. She was still wearing slacks and a sweater. But her hair
was in disarray, as if she hadn't checked herself in the mirror for
a few hours. She stood there, waiting for Manny, not trying to run.

Manny got out slowly, warily, looking around as if he expected
an ambush. He wore gray slacks and a black silk shirt, and carried
a blue-and-white flight bag in one hand. By the way he swung it,
I could tell it wasn't empty. He joined Vivian at the front of the
car, grabbed her arm just above the elbow, and led her away.

I went after them.

But when I reached the edge of the parking area, they were
gone.

The entrance to the theater was at least a hundred yards away;
they couldn't have made it there already. I counted a dozen or so
park visitors—four teenagers, a young couple with a child, and a
group of six that included the grandparents.

Where the hell were Vivian and Manny?

Then I spotted them to my right, just off the parking area.
Vivian sat on a bench with her back to me, facing a void. A
thousand feet down-slope from her lay a gravel parking lot the

size of three football fields. In the distance the front range marched away to the south.

Manny was crouched before the bench. I saw him peel away a sheet of paper that must have been taped underneath. A message from Blyleven? Manny scanned it, then impatiently crumpled it up and tossed it aside. He took Vivian by the arm and walked her toward the amphitheater's entrance. He glanced this way and that, sharp little head movements, like a hawk on the lookout for mice. It was too risky to take him now.

And where was Blyleven?

I kept my eye on them, hustled over to the bench, and retrieved the wadded paper.

The sheet had been torn from a spiral notebook. The message was printed in pencil, block letters, all caps:

SIT IN FRONT ROW CENTER
WATCH THE STAGE

I jogged across the parking area to an asphalt pathway. It led around the end of a towering red rock wall to the amphitheater's entrance. A hundred feet overhead swallows soared and darted about the rock face.

I hustled down the gently sloping, curving path, meeting tourists coming up. Manny and Vivian had already reached the end of the path. They disappeared behind a concession stand built from native rock.

When I got there, I was standing at the top of the theater.

There were twenty or so people scattered about. There was room for eight thousand more. The seats were wide, backless benches, curving in a semicircle, a few hundred feet from end to end, and seventy steep rows to the bottom. Concrete steps descended beyond the ends of the rows. And beyond the steps were sheer rock walls, bracketing the theater, keeping in the sound. Another, shorter rock wall, maybe thirty feet high and a hundred feet long, ran along the rear of the stage, far below. Miles behind the stage I could just make out the tiny towers of downtown Denver.

Manny and Vivian were going down the steps along the left side of the theater.

When they got about a third of the way down, they suddenly stopped. Manny turned, searching faces, as alert and cautious as a mountain cat.

I sat quickly near a small group of tourists and bent down as if to tie my shoe.

After a few minutes Manny seemed satisfied. He ushered Vivian down the stone steps. When they reached the bottom row, they walked to the middle, and sat. Manny held the flight bag in his lap.

On the stage before them three youngsters played hackey-sack. I was too far away to see the little leather bag, but the kids' movements couldn't have been for anything else. Is this what Blyleven wanted them to watch?

Thunder rumbled behind me, like oil drums tumbling down a mountain slope. A tiny raindrop hit my forehead.

Where was Blyleven?

I made a quick tally of everyone in sight. No more than two dozen people were scattered about, including my six neighbors, two of whom were from Denver, telling their friends from Iowa about the last concert they'd seen here.

Then one guy caught my eye.

He was sitting alone at the other end of my row, two hundred feet from me. He wore a dark blue ball cap, matching windbreaker, and khaki pants. He was leaning forward, hands on knees, staring intently at the stage below. Or maybe at Vivian and Manny. I was too far away to make out his features, but from photographs I'd seen, he was the same size and build as Blyleven.

Now he scanned the people in the seats, taking his time, appraising each person.

He was Blyleven, all right.

When he looked my way, I leaned over and asked the Denver guy where Pike's Peak was. The guy pointed south, in the general direction of Blyleven.

"It's over that way," he said, "but you can't see it from here."

Blyleven continued to study each person in the amphitheater. Then, suddenly, he lurched to his feet and began walking quickly down the steps. The bill of his cap was pointed directly at the middle of the front row.

I went after him. I planned to grab him before he confronted Manny, maybe even trade him to Manny for Vivian.

But by the time I'd sprinted along the two-hundred-foot row to the steps, Blyleven was already near the bottom. I ran down the steps, then turned into the seats about twenty rows up from the bottom, so I could approach them all from directly behind.

As I clambered down the seats, Blyleven came up behind Vivian and Manny, a gun in his hand. I saw Manny turn around. He stood and offered the bag. Blyleven reached for it. Quick as a snake, Manny grabbed Blyleven's gun hand and swung the bag overhand, hitting Blyleven in the face, knocking him backward. The gun clattered to the concrete. Blyleven took off running.

I yelled, "Hold it!"

Manny either didn't hear me or didn't care. He ran after Blyleven. He still had the flight bag. As he ran, he jerked it open, pulled out a chunky black automatic weapon, and tossed the bag aside.

I shouted at Vivian, "Call the police!" But she looked too stunned to move.

I ran after Manny and Blyleven.

They were already past the end of the stage, sprinting out the right side of the amphitheater, Blyleven a few dozen yards in the lead.

I scrambled down a flight of steps that ended at a sloping asphalt ramp. It curved down and around the huge wall of rock. Blyleven was already out of sight. I watched Manny disappear around the curve. Then I heard a metallic clatter as he fired his weapon.

I rounded the curve, yanking the .357 from my shoulder holster.

Manny had just reached the bottom of the ramp, fifty feet from me. Blyleven was in the open, sprinting into a vast gravel parking area toward a lone car. He could run, but he couldn't hide. Manny stopped and held the weapon at arm's length.

I shouted at him.

Manny fired a burst. It cut Blyleven down.

Now Manny swung around toward me, firing, spraying bullets off the rock face.

I was braced, arms extended, gun in both hands, sights aligned between his elbows and his shoulders. Before he got all the way around, I shot him once, the magnum bucking angrily in my hands. Manny's shoulders slumped, and he stumbled toward me, trying to keep from falling. He struggled to raise the weapon. I shot him again. He let go of the gun and fell to his knees. Then he crumpled facedown on the ramp.

I moved toward him cautiously, keeping my piece pointed at his head. It didn't matter. He was dead.

I picked up the chunky black TEC-9 by the trigger guard and carried it down to where Blyleven lay in the gravel. He was on his back, his cap gone and blood oozing out of him.

At least he wasn't dead.

Then again, he wasn't Blyleven.

An old burn scar covered his neck and chin. Stan Lessing.

33

Stan Lessing lay still, staring up at me. I knelt beside him in the gravel.

"I can't move," he said.

His voice was a harsh whisper—weak, but surprisingly calm, considering. Probably going into shock. I peeled off my jacket, laid it over his chest, and pulled it up to his chin. His khaki pants were black with blood from the crotch to the belt. I put my hand under his head for a little comfort. Gravel bit into my skin.

"Don't worry, Stan, we'll get an ambulance."

"How . . . how do you know my name?"

I saw Vivian rushing down the ramp. She stopped dead in her tracks when she saw Manny's body, thirty yards from me and Stan. I figured she'd either faint, throw up, or go back the way she came. Instead, she hurried forward and knelt beside Manny. Then she started going through the dead man's pockets, like a ghoul.

"Vivian, go call the police. Tell them we need an ambulance."

She pulled a set of keys from Manny's pants pocket. Then she stood, trembling. Her face was bone white. "Is Martin . . . here?"

"No. Go call the police."

"Chelsea and Roger," she said. "They're locked in the trunk of the car." She turned her back on me and Stan and hurried up the ramp to free her family.

"How do you know my name?" Stan asked again.

"I know a lot about you," I said. "And about your scheming with Martin Blyleven."

"The bastard double-crossed me."

It was starting to rain now, a light drizzle. Thunder growled above the nearby hills. I brushed my hand across Stan's forehead to keep moisture from running in his eyes.

"Where's Blyleven?"

"Dead." Stan licked his lips, and then he winced. He tried to look down at his wounds.

"Just lie still," I said.

"Is it bad?"

"I'm no doctor."

"Am I . . . going to die?"

"We're all going to die, Stan."

"Tell me."

"It looks pretty goddamn bad."

A few young guys came into sight around the curve in the ramp. They moved hesitantly toward Manny's body, gawking, as if it had fallen from a UFO.

"Go call the police!" I shouted at them. "And an ambulance!"

One of them stepped gingerly around Manny's body, then ran along the gravel driveway that led from the parking lot to the curio shop, out of sight beyond the rocks.

"How did you find out about us?" Stan asked.

"I talked to everyone, including your ex-girlfriend, and pieced it together. Most of it, anyway."

Stan smiled weakly. "How is Debbie?"

"About the same," I said. I didn't remind him that he'd abandoned her when she was pregnant. Or tell him that he had a daughter. Debbie could do that, if he survived.

"She's a good woman," Stan said. "Better off without me."

"Maybe. Tell me how Blyleven died."

He licked his lips and winced. "It's a long story."

"We have some time."

He tried to smile. "You wouldn't believe me."

"Tell me anyway."

He did. Why not? What else did he have to do?

As he talked, tourists drifted down from the amphitheater. Most of them took one look at Manny's body and went back up the ramp. A few made it over to me and Stan. They kept their distance, though, no doubt put off by the sight of Stan's blood soaking into the ground.

Stan told me that Blyleven figured out how to get away with stealing the mob's money when he first saw Stan's scars. A body burned beyond recognition, that was the idea.

They'd met at the chess club and swapped army stories. When Blyleven learned that Stan had been in Special Forces, he knew the expertise he needed was at hand. He brought Stan in as a full partner. Supposedly. Stan taught Blyleven how to rig explosives and how to operate a parachute.

One other thing Stan taught him—how to kill a man.

It was a pretty problem. The pilot would have to be killed after the plane was airborne and the controls were put on automatic pilot. And he'd have to be killed quickly. If he struggled or thrashed around, he might hit the controls and knock the plane off course.

Also, Blyleven wanted it to look as if the pilot had died in the explosion. In other words, no gunshot wounds.

Stan's solution was an ice pick.

"Slam it into a guy's head," Stan said weakly. "Ninety-nine times out of a hundred he drops dead. And all it leaves is a tiny hole in the skull. Who'd notice that after the plane blew up?"

Blyleven had made arrangements for phony IDs, passports, and airline tickets from Los Angeles to Mexico City with connections to Brazil.

"For *both* of us," Stan said. "I was supposed to meet him in LA."

Blyleven had calculated where to jump—a spot about twenty miles from Holbrook, Arizona, near the Petrified Forest. The area was remote enough that Blyleven wouldn't be seen, especially if he jumped at twilight. And the terrain wasn't so rugged that he couldn't hike out.

The week before the flight, they took Stan's car to Holbrook and paid cash to some old-timer to store it in his shed.

The night before the flight, they went to the hangar at Centennial Airport to load the plane—high explosives, a parachute, and a cadaver that Blyleven supposedly had acquired from a medical school and stashed in a rubber body bag in the trunk of his car.

Of course, there was no cadaver. Stan would fill that role.

When they carried the explosives into the plane, Blyleven used the ice pick on Stan.

"It should have killed me," Stan whispered. "But it didn't. One side of my face was paralyzed for months, but otherwise . . ."

The force of the blow knocked Stan unconscious. He woke up in the plane's storage compartment.

Then he waited.

The plane took off the next afternoon. Some hours later, Blyleven slammed the ice pick into Lawrence Foster's head. This time it worked. He went to the rear of the plane to drag Stan's body from the compartment. Stan was ready. He jumped Blyleven and killed him, breaking his neck. Then he rigged the explosives to his former partner, put on the parachute, clutched the briefcase filled with cash, and waited for the landmarks.

After he bailed out, he spent the night in the desert, wrapped in the silk parachute. Before dawn, he buried the chute and began the twenty-mile hike to Holbrook. It took him all day. He followed a road, ducking behind rocks whenever an occasional car appeared.

"I drove my car to Mexico." Stan's voice had grown steadily weaker. I had to lean down to hear him. "Maybe I should have stuck to Blyleven's original plan," he said, "because after that, everything turned to shit."

Somewhere in central Mexico Stan was stopped by the local police. He spoke little Spanish, and he may have misunderstood what they wanted. But rather than risking arrest, he offered them a bribe.

They took it.

In fact, they took the entire briefcase filled with money. Then they beat him half to death, partially crushing his larynx, and threw him in a territorial prison. Three years later he managed to escape. It took him another year to make his way back to the States.

"Those Mexican cops were probably living the high life in Acapulco," Stan whispered, "and I was destitute in El Paso."

He stole money and a car, and he drove to Colorado. Blyleven had told him a lot about Vivian and Chelsea—including that he'd left them with a fat insurance policy. Stan decided to try to get it.

"I figured I deserved it." His voice was so weak now that I could hardly hear him. There was blood in his spittle. "What do you think?"

"Maybe so, Stan."

He died before help arrived.

By then there were a dozen or so people standing around us in the rain. Including Roger Armis. The rain was coming down steadily now, a heavy drizzle that had already soaked my clothes. I resisted the urge to put on my jacket. Instead, I pulled it up over Stan's face.

A sheriff's car rolled into the lot, lights flashing. Roger Armis stepped forward and started to say something to me.

I stood and said, "Everybody make room for the cops. Go on, get out of here." I pushed Armis in the chest and held his eyes with mine. "All of you get out of here. None of this concerns you."

He hesitated. Then he turned and walked away. Everyone else stayed.

34

I danced around with the county sheriff and the Denver cops for the next few days. I kept repeating my story:

Manny kidnapped me and locked me in the truck of my car. He said he was going to meet Blyleven at Red Rocks and kill him. Then he was going to kill me. After he parked my car, I managed to escape from the trunk. Luckily, I kept a gun in there. I chased Manny. He shot the man with the scar. When he tried to shoot me, I killed him in self-defense.

The sheriff didn't like it.

Lieutenant Dalrymple hated it.

But the physical evidence seemed to fit the facts. And really, no one was crying over the demise of Manny Mancusso. As for the man with the scar, they could only speculate who he was—his car and ID were both stolen. I figured that eventually they'd identify him through his fingerprints and army record. But nobody would really care. Not even Debbie Ogborn.

Finally, the police let me go.

The Reverend Franklin Reed exposed World Flock in a special televised sermon. He wept openly, baring his soul before God and the camera. He asked his parishioners to forgive him. They did. The collection plates were passed without further delay.

The police more or less forgave Reed, too, granting him immunity in return for turning state's evidence. Matthew Styles, however, was ostracized by the church council and left alone to face charges of money laundering and fraud.

In Tucson, the lawyers for Joseph Scolla had no comment.

I phoned Roger Armis to tell him the situation was over. I also wanted to know how he and his family were getting along.

Thankfully, Chelsea wasn't experiencing any post trauma from their brief encounter with Manny. Of course, her dad had been there to comfort her—even when locked in the trunk of the family car. Vivian, though, was still shaken by the recent events. She was receiving counseling. Roger was grateful that I hadn't brought her to the attention of the police.

"There was no reason," I said.

"Yes, I suppose you're right. Besides, Vivian has suffered enough."

We both knew she'd suffer more. She'd have to live with the certain knowledge that her first husband had deceived her, used her in an attempt to steal money, and murdered Lawrence Foster with an ice pick.

It was this last fact that caused me some concern.

Should I tell Nora Foster? As far as she knew, her husband had died in an unexplained midair explosion. Would it help her to know the truth—that he'd already been dead when the plane blew up, a sliver of metal rammed into his brain?

Somehow, I doubted it.

Still, I called her. Although it took me a few days to work up the nerve. Not because of her. As I said, I've never been too good with kids. But what the hell, maybe I should try harder.

"I'd like to pay you back," I told her.

"For what?"

"The dinner last week."

"Don't be silly."

"Well, I have three tickets to the Rockies game this Sunday. Would you and Brian like to go?"

"Oh, Brian would love it."

"Brian. Well, good."

"And so would I," she said. I could hear the smile in her voice.

Oh, by the way, Mrs. Finch evicted Sharon Hoffman. The apartment's still vacant, if you know anyone who's interested.